The Museum of Us

The
Museum
of
Us

TARA WILSON REDD

Text copyright © 2018 by Tara Wilson Redd
Jacket sky background art by Shutterstock
Jacket couple photograph © 2018 by Stephen Carroll/Trevillion Images
Jacket design by Whitney Manger

All rights reserved. Published in the United States by Wendy Lamb Books, an imprint of Random House Children's Books, a division of Penguin Random House LLC, New York.

Wendy Lamb Books and the colophon are trademarks of Penguin Random House LLC.

Visit us on the Web! GetUnderlined.com

Educators and librarians, for a variety of teaching tools, visit us at RHTeachersLibrarians.com

Library of Congress Cataloging-in-Publication Data
Name: Redd, Tara Wilson, author.
Title: The museum of us / Tara Wilson Redd.
Description: First edition. | New York : Wendy Lamb Books, an imprint of Random House Children's Books, [2018] | Summary: "Sixteen-year-old Sadie is lucky to survive an accident, but it changes her world forever when it reveals her secret life and the mysterious, thrilling boy at the center of it." — Provided by publisher. | Identifiers: LCCN 2017028438 (print) | LCCN 2017040127 (ebook) | ISBN 978-1-5247-6689-4 (ebook) | ISBN 978-1-5247-6687-0 (hardcover) | ISBN 978-1-5247-6688-7 (lib. bdg.) | ISBN 978-1-5247-6690-0 (pbk.)
Subjects: | CYAC: Medical care—Fiction. | Hospitals—Fiction. | Imaginary friends—Fiction. | Psychotherapy—Fiction. | Mental illness—Fiction. | Automobile accidents—Fiction.
Classification: LCC PZ7.1.R3998 (ebook) | LCC PZ7.1.R3998 Mus 2018 (print) | DDC [Fic]—dc23

The text of this book is set in 12.6-point Granjon LT Std.
Interior design by Jaclyn Whalen

Printed in the United States of America
10 9 8 7 6 5 4 3 2 1
First Edition

For my parents, David and Tina

For Alexander, always

THE BOY WHO LEFT

George's blue eyes captured her. They were dark as the deep blue sea and Sadie was adrift under a starless night. No going back now.

Sadie turned the ignition key and revved her truck, Old Charlotte, to life. The air-conditioning raised goose bumps on her skin. It was one hundred degrees outside but she was cold. She checked her phone one last time: two texts—one from Lucie and one from Henry—and a voice mail from her parents. George rustled the maps in his lap and raised an eyebrow at her, so she tossed her phone into the glove compartment. George grabbed her wrist and kissed the palm of her hand, closing the glove box with the toe of his impeccably shined shoe.

It had taken her three tries, private lessons, and eight months to get her license. Being behind the wheel was still strange and exciting and scary.

She glanced at his maps. The whole pile was marked with red Sharpie. "Anyone with a true sense of adventure knows how to read a map. You have to imagine the world that goes with it," George had told her. "GPS is the death of imagination." So they'd spent last night lying side by side on the filthy basement rug dreaming up interesting destinations. They'd lost themselves in more exotic fantasies in Sadie's many purloined atlases—Rio, Morocco, and always, always Moscow—but they weren't going to be driving to Russia in a beat-up Ford F100, no matter how beautifully her parents had restored their truck, dear Old Charlotte.

The limits of reality turned dreams back into paper maps. Even with a car, you couldn't really escape. Mapped out, the landmarks of Sadie's life made such a small circle: her parents' repair shop, Henry's house, the library, school. She would be a senior in the fall, but that didn't expand her life into unknown territory. The colleges she hoped to visit in the fall were in-state. A tiny world.

George had seen her disappointment. He'd tried to make it better. Even in St. Louis, with George there were adventures. "Let me give you one perfect day," he had begged, and he'd drawn their adventure right there on the map. He circled destination after destination, linking them with one red line. "A bright red line toward destiny," he had called it.

And now they were on that red line.

George slid on his Clubmasters, the dark lenses a villainous mask. He smiled and looked away, eighteen years of cultivated cool settling into a leather seat. His smile destroyed her. He didn't have to grow up to be someone; he already was someone.

Sadie put on her Ray-Ban knockoffs. On the floor, her polka-dot backpack was filled with snacks and books and her still-shiny driver's license. The backpack sat between George's black shoes, his black briefcase nestled beside it, holding whatever mysteries he'd packed away with his imported cigarettes. Old Charlotte was rumbling in anticipation, but Sadie gripped the steering wheel with clammy hands, her foot on the brake, toeing the clutch.

A night of maps had seemed so far away from this plan.

George put his hand on the steering wheel over hers. "To seek and find?"

His voice washed away all doubt.

"To seek and find," she replied, putting the truck in gear with an audible creak.

It was easy. Time slipped by them, unnoticed. The radio was broken, but it didn't matter. George told her stories. He sang Beatles songs—at least, the parts he could remember, making up the rest. She didn't care. Nothing could ruin this day.

As the sun climbed the sky, they settled into the comfortable silence of the oldest of friends. They split a burger and milk shake. They stopped at the art museum, the history museum, the zoo. There was a whole world in Forest Park. Back in the truck, George fell asleep as Sadie drove home under a perfect sunset, his long legs buckled under him like a contortionist. He smelled like cigarettes and bourbon and looked so much like a little boy.

I will never love anyone this much, thought Sadie, stealing glances at him as he slept. She retreated into that thought and fell into the memories of him, into their inseparable future together.

She didn't even see the tree.

✳

Moments passed like snapshots being thrown into the trash:

The summer light filtered through green oak leaves.

The drip of a melted pink milk shake falling sideways.

The crushed door papered with bloodied maps.

The shimmer of blue broken glass diamonds.

The bone sticking out of her leg.

The empty seat beside her.

✳

Sadie was alone. The taste of blood faded and was replaced with the certainty that she was dying. She felt like she was seeing the world from the bottom of the ocean. She couldn't hear herself screaming, though she knew she was. All she could hear was the icy note of tragedy, like the dead sound people hear after a bomb.

Then she wasn't alone. People, strangers, were all around her. Hands were on her face, and more hands tied her down. But she needed to sit up. She needed to find him. She closed her eyes tight and when she opened them, she was in a different place. *Am I dreaming, or dead?* she thought in a panic. Lights went by and blinded her. Everyone was talking. She could tell they were trying to talk to her, but she couldn't make out what they were saying.

An emergency room, she realized. She tried to get up and run, but her legs wouldn't obey. She was trapped.

"George," she said, over and over. "Where is George?"

DAY 1

Today is Day 1 of my captivity.

I add "Day 1" right at the top of the page. I stop. I don't know what else to write. My thoughts wander, and my pen makes a kind of out-of-control swirl right below the words until it runs off the page.

Dr. Roberts gave me this notebook. I'm supposed to write my thoughts in it. I told her: "Fine. In exchange I will get my phone back."

Dr. Roberts just shrugged. She knows my phone is in a million pieces in what remains of Old Charlotte (may she rest in peace).

I knew that too, but I didn't want to give away something for nothing. That's not what a spy would do. But that's how this started; otherwise I wouldn't be writing this down at all.

I try to focus. I stare hard at the paper. Thoughts are nothing. Writing it down makes it real.

I just want to get out of here. This is all a stupid mistake.

I haven't even filled one sheet of paper yet. There are pages and pages between me and freedom.

If today is Day 1, then yesterday was Day Zero: kind of like the zero point, which is the point of detonation of a nuclear bomb. The zero point can be in the air, underwater, in outer space, wherever. When something blows up, the zero point is where it happens. From there, you can measure out in concentric circles and look at the impact. The farther away you go, the less impact there is.

But time isn't like space, exactly. And the thing about "trauma" (which is what everyone keeps calling my *accident*) is that it's not a bomb that blows up once. Just thinking about it brings it back again and again. You can be years from Day Zero and find yourself right back at the point of origin. Unlike a bomb in space, a bomb in time has a gravitational pull. It bends time, taking you with it. I was in a car crash yesterday, and I was in a car crash five years ago. These things have nothing to do with each other, and I've explained that, but I can understand how it might look like they do. I don't even remember the other crash. Not really. But people want to find patterns. Reasons why.

I look down. My pen is resting on the page.

I'm supposed to be writing. What have I been doing?

Thinking. When I'm thinking I'm completely lost.

Well, this is an awful start to a journal. I suck at diaries because I have nothing to put in them. I've thrown away every journal I've ever written in because they were worthless. I'm always so embarrassed to have thought that my life was worth writing about that I rip out the pages, burn them with a lighter, and then bury the hollow shell in a trash can in Blackburn Park so maybe it can have some peace while it decomposes far away from me. And I think maybe if someone found the empty shell of a journal sitting with all those brown bagged bottles in a park trash can, they might pick it up and wonder what it held: first my Hogwarts crest one, then my purple one with the little heart lock, then the one I had in ninth grade that said SADIE in gold on the front. People have been giving me journals my whole life, and I've failed to live up to every single one.

Right now I'm writing in this floppy green one-subject Mead notebook Dr. Roberts pulled out of her briefcase full of the lives of other people. It's different paper but the same old story. See, if you found one of my gutted journals and wondered what important secrets had been ripped out of it, you'd just be furthering the illusion that someone important wrote in it. Even throwing away my journals is just one more way that I'm a big melodramatic liar, trying to make something sound important that isn't.

I know the truth: nothing was ever in that journal at all, because nothing was ever in that life at all.

I pick up my pen.

Here are the three most interesting things about me,
Sadie Black:

1) I was homeschooled until middle school because my
   parents traveled a lot for car shows, because
2) Said parents were formerly local radio celebrities
   (emphasis on local) with a show about antique cars
   and antique music, which is ironic because
3) Five years ago they were driving one of said antique
   cars and listening to said antique music when we got
   in the car accident that made the local news.

See? In the grand scheme of the universe, I'm pretty boring. I'm not even a National Honor Society member. I'm
writing in this worthless little journal because my worthless
little self crashed a worthless little truck for no reason into
nothing. (Actually into a tree. The tree was real.)

How's that for melodrama?

Melodramas were a popular type of film in the golden
age of Hollywood. They are usually defined as exagger-
ated films that play on the emotions of the audience, often
with stereotyped characters: an evil doctor, oblivious parents, a knight in shining armor, young lovers destined for
doomed love. They made loads of money because women
absolutely adored them. They were sometimes even called
women's weepies. *Gone with the Wind, Casablanca,* and my
favorite, *Now, Voyager,* are all melodramas.

I love melodrama because you don't mean it, and then
you do. It's ridiculous, and then it's not. You think you're

laughing at it, and then you're crying. Being sixteen is a melodrama (she thinks, melodramatically).

Do I mean it, or don't I? I don't even know. I don't know if I'm the person in my head or the mask I wear to get by in the real world.

I try one last time:

I feel like nothing and all of this is about nothing and no one will ever read it.

I feel all the anger, the bad things, rising out of the past and down into my fingertips. I press hard into the page.

Except you, Dr. Roberts. I know you're reading this. You specifically said that you wouldn't, but I bet anything you are. I know how these things work. Stay out of my notebook.

If I weren't so angry, I would rescind my previous statement about Dr. Roberts. Maybe I'd rip out the page, or just cross it out. I mean, maybe Roberts wouldn't read my journal. As far as psychiatrists go, she's not the most heinous quasi quack I've ever met. And I've met quite a few: my parents were "concerned" after the first accident, and last year my school was "concerned" when I started failing my classes. But whenever someone is "concerned" I just go into self-preservation mode, get my act together, put on my normal-person mask, and fake my way back to acceptable human behavior.

I've had journals before. I'm not stupid: nothing anyone writes is really, truly a secret. The second you uncap a pen, you've already lost. Secrets are con artists: they trick you into letting them out. I know better than to write the truth in a journal. Your mind is the only vault you can trust.

But can you even trust that?

I can't even keep track of the time.

How can I keep track of my secrets?

✳

Dr. Roberts comes in to talk with me.

"When you were brought in, Sadie, do you remember what you were saying?"

And I think, *How could I have been so careless? How could I have been so stupid?*

"You kept talking about a friend of yours. George?"

"No, I don't think so."

"Well, the thing is, this George . . . was he injured? Was he in the car with you?"

"No," I tell her. *Nonononononono,* I scream in my head. Because how could this be happening? And I'm still so messed up from the crash and everything, I can almost see George standing next to Dr. Roberts, like he's coming to save me. But I know he couldn't possibly be there, so I don't say anything to him.

"Can you tell me, who is George?" she asks.

Panic sucks me into darkness.

"He's nobody," I say.

"Well, if you think of anything, be sure to write it down. In fact, just write down whatever you're thinking about. We often underestimate what trauma can shatter. You never know what's going to be important. Sometimes memories come back in pieces after an accident," she reminds me.

Write it down. She wants me to write it down. What will that do? It won't change anything. But like an idiot, I try again once she leaves.

I remember . . .

But I don't remember. Not really. I don't remember what *really* happened. I just remember how it *felt* to me. And that's too dangerous to put in writing.

But I guess it's my chance to contest the picture Dr. Roberts is painting in the notes she takes. My chance to fight back before my parents get home from Germany tomorrow. Sort out the lies I'm going to tell. My story in her notes scares me. I don't know what she's saying. She's got a big legal pad she writes on, and when we were done talking yesterday she put the pages away in her briefcase with about a million other files. Schizophrenics and kleptomaniacs and suicidal people . . . and me.

Her briefcase is actually nice. It's the box kind, almost

like George's. George carries an Ettinger attaché case with red lining. I cut out a picture of exactly the right one from a newspaper in the library. I should definitely not have mutilated library property, but how could I not? It was perfect.

George loves that case. Whatever adventure we're on, it's stocked. I've seen him pull a gun out of it, a book of spells, roses, the keys to an Aston Martin DB5. . . . I imagine him now, fiddling with the lock he broke ages ago, looking at me with adventure written in his eyes.

Click goes the attaché case. I wonder what he has in store for me today.

I imagine it, but I can't write that down.

But then, what difference does it make? This kind of thing does not simply go away without an explanation. Not when there's property damage and insurance claims involved.

I am stuck between the devil and the deep blue sea, as Dad would say. Write it down and they'll think I'm crazy. Don't write it down and I'll look like I have something to hide.

Well, if I've learned anything from explorers and detectives, it's that the very best journals aren't full of confessions, they're full of observations. When you go on adventures, you don't have to fill your journal pages with mopey thoughts about boys and gossip and self-indulgent, self-pitying *feelings*. When you're amazing, you just write down the things you saw and did and that's enough.

Maybe I'm not exactly on a quest, but I won't bore myself with feelings and confessions, even though that's what Dr. Roberts obviously wants. Instead, here is what I observe:

I am in St. Louis Children's Hospital, which I know because of the bright, friendly decorating and the giant signs that say that basically everywhere.

Not exactly Sherlock Holmes–level deduction, that one.

My loaner pajamas have small bears on them. My room has no phone, limited television stations, and blue curtains. No room-mates. There's some kind of a desk where the nurses sit down the hall, presumably with a line of sight past my door. This would be more relevant to any fantasy of escape if I could walk. My leg is in a cast, and I know, somewhere in my brain under an ocean of morphine, it hurts like hell. I have been isolated, but I never seem to be alone. There's always someone with me or checking on me, every second, every hour, even into the night.

All those things are real. All those things are true. I observed them and wrote them down. I know the difference between real and pretend, and that is how I know that I am not insane. No matter what they tell me, I'm not crazy.

Because, you see, Dr. Roberts is a psychiatrist—*that* I remember—and it's no accident that she's been interrogating me. And that is not good. That is not good at all.

I will admit to one feeling: I'm scared I'm really in trouble this time.

Oh God, I miss George.

It used to be if I couldn't fall asleep, I would spend those hours with him. Going out on weird little missions, or sitting around talking about nothing. We would walk around in the afterthought of humidity that clings to these St. Louis days. In the suburbs, the streets are safe and cool, and there's never anyone outside after midnight. My bedroom in the basement is great for that. You can creep out the cellar door without a sound. My room doesn't have any windows, so I take a lot of naps during the day. I sleep a lot, and then I can't sleep when I'm supposed to, but the plus side is that I never have to be awake with everyone else either.

I can't even think of George here, let alone go anywhere with him. Sometimes my mind starts to wander and I can feel myself slipping and him pulling at me, but then I notice and snap out of it. Because what if someone saw me? What if someone saw the empty shell that keeps me tethered to this world, its lips moving and smiling while the real me is somewhere else?

I'm here alone in the dark and I don't know what to do.

I feel like crying, but tears won't bring him back. That's what Ole Golly said in *Harriet the Spy*. I read that book a million times when I was younger, and it was like Ole Golly herself was there with me, guiding me. But you know, Ole Golly leaves Harriet in that book, for no good reason. And

Harriet just has to accept that, and I never liked that part of the story. So I would pretend she actually was coming back right after the book ended, even though that's not the point.

"Your parents will be here first thing tomorrow," Dr. Roberts tells me. I wake up. I've been lost in thought. How did she get here? How long have we been talking? "They're on their way from Germany now." I know I talked to them when they called, but I can't remember. Everything is hazy and weird.

"Are they taking me home?"

"Not quite yet. Tomorrow we're going to move you out of this room and into another ward, where we can give you more of the attention you need."

"Because of my leg?"

"No, because of your mind."

That is such an amazing villain line. It sounds so evil, even though she probably thinks she's being gentle. That makes it even more villainous, that knife twist of kindness.

"Sadie, do you remember what we've been talking about?" she asks. I nod, even though I don't.

"You'll see. It'll be good to have a few days' rest."

"My parents will take me home."

"It's already been discussed, Sadie. You're spending a few days here with us, in a controlled environment, just until we're sure everything's okay."

"What do you mean 'everything'?"

"That's what we're going to find out," she replies. "We have a lot to talk about with your parents. But when you and I talk, everything we say is completely confidential. Absolutely private. And I know you don't want to talk about this, but I need you to tell me about George. Did he hurt you? Are you afraid? No one can get to you here, Sadie. You can tell me about George."

And there it is. The one thing I can't tell her. The one thing I must never write down.

It's all coming down around me. I need to get out of here, and I need to keep my secret. George is both my devil and my deep blue sea. He's the one key to my freedom. They want to know who he is and where he went and why I was screaming his name after the crash.

And the reason I can't answer any of that, of course, is because George isn't real.

OCCLUMENCY

George and Sadie knew the Hogwarts Library the way only two Ravenclaws could. Tricks were for Gryffindors. They needed no Invisibility Cloak to sneak around after dark into the stacks. They knew the whorls in the dust, the moonlight glint off every pane of stained glass, and most important, the exact location of the book they needed to pass through the next task of the Triwizard Tournament.

"Over here!" Sadie whispered. She climbed up a rolling ladder without a creak. The spines were dusty, but she could still make out the titles.

"Hang on, this is the missing volume of the *Book of Memory* I was looking for last week," George said, distracted by a dusty tome that had been abandoned on a cart. "Damned disrespectful. This is the one with all the methods for countering Obliviate, and all the truly scary memory spells as well. You could change the past with this, you know. See, if absolutely no one remembered something, it would be like it never happened. No wonder it's in the restricted section."

"George, we haven't time for this." George rolled his eyes. Her posh accent made her sound like an insufferable know-it-all.

"Well, I'm certainly putting it back where it belongs, anyway. They really ought to put all this in order."

"George! This is not the time—"

"What are you doing in here?" the nurse asked. Sadie fell back into her hospital room and snapped to attention. Her mouth was still full of words she had been mumbling to no one. The nurse paused in the doorway, then came into Sadie's room to look around.

"Nothing," Sadie muttered, her face burning. "I wasn't doing anything."

"Who were you talking to?"

"No one. I wasn't . . . Can I just go to bed now?" The nurse raised an eyebrow.

"That sounds like a good idea. It's late, Sadie. You go to sleep now. Don't make me come back in here."

The nurse flipped off the lights and Sadie's head spun with panic. Her heart pounded as she contemplated how close she'd come to letting someone see her talking with George. She'd almost been caught, and it was worse than ever: she didn't even remember when she'd drifted into the fantasy. In the dark, she couldn't focus on the room around her. All she could think about was herself and her feelings.

Her leg ached inside its cast, and the rest of her itched under unfamiliar covers. She wanted her own pajamas. She wanted her own room. She closed her eyes and felt tears seeping out onto her pillow.

She wanted to go home to George.

But she couldn't. It wasn't safe.

Instead, she closed her eyes and in her head recited all the Beatles songs she knew by heart. She focused on each line, like praying. She prayed her way through album after album, tear after tear escaping her sleepy eyes.

Her eyes closed, she heard the sound of a lighter flipping open, then igniting.

"Are we alone?" George asked, revealed behind the door as he pushed it closed. He lit his cigarette, and smoke began to fill the room.

"George!" she cried. She sprang out of bed, and when she wrapped her arms around him, he seemed so thin under his suit, like he was barely there. "You came," she whimpered into his chest.

"Of course I came, darling. But we need to be careful. You don't know what they'll do to us. What they'll do to you."

"Don't leave me," Sadie begged. "Please. Don't leave me alone here."

"All right, darling, all right. Let's go somewhere we can talk." She held him tighter and he let out a moan. She inspected him in the dim light. Had he been injured in the crash?

But the moment she began to notice all his scars and bruises—a lifetime of pain—they were gone. His face was as clean and smooth and pale and young as it always had been.

"Where should we go?" Sadie asked.

"I don't know. Somewhere far away," George said. He grabbed her hand. "Darling, we have to run as far from here as we can get."

✳

In the black nothing—the same nothing at the start of every story—George tapped his fingernails on the side of his rocks glass. The music of it broke through the darkness, creating the world around them note by note. The whole world started with George.

Sadie took a sip of tea from her little blue cup. It was broken with cracks of gold. *Kintsugi,* she recalled, was the name for it: a broken cup made whole, better than before. She could smell the whiskey in George's cocktail: an old-fashioned.

Where had they traveled now? She had grown used to figuring out their universe as she wandered through it. Sometimes she wondered if she created the world by seeing it, or if it had always been there waiting to be seen. George belonged automatically wherever they went. He was forever the same—eighteen and beautiful—but somehow placeless and timeless. Sadie always had to decide who she would be. She could be an explorer, or a princess, or a spy. Anything. This time, she felt like she might be stuck as herself.

She wrapped her hospital gown around her until it felt like a straitjacket. "Something terrible is happening, George. I just can't remember what."

"I know," George said, but offered no help.

She took a deep breath, another sip of tea, and began the revelation of the world.

They were sitting in a small room with a glass wall on one side that peered out into darkness. She couldn't see any farther than the candlelight from their table, where her beautiful tea set reconfigured with gold stood next to George's cocktail torture implements: strainers and stabbers and spoons and all sorts of tools she wasn't quite sure how to use. The room was small and dim, with black fleur-de-lis wallpaper cut from the set of some BBC drama she couldn't quite place. There were no doors, but the walls were lined with bookshelves. In gold on one of the aging leather spines, she could make out a faded title: *The Wizard Prince and the Book of Memory.*

The candlelight isn't enough to see anything, she thought. As though answering her, a chandelier above them began to glow. She looked up as the Edison bulbs lit their eerie filaments, the light flooding the small room and the place beyond the glass.

Sadie stood and went to the window. It looked out into a hall lined with rooms much like their own: little glass prisons. Their dim lights faintly illuminated the cells.

The room across the hall held her favorite corner of the Hogwarts library, a dusty book lying open on the table. The wind leafed through its pages and snuffed the candle out. The room next to that was a squalid safe house they'd once used in Moscow. On the other side, she spied the outside of a café she knew in Rio, normally a bustling spot. Drinks sat out as though all the customers had stepped away only moments ago.

All the rooms were empty sets. The hairs on her arms stood up. Not a soul was there. She and George were all alone.

George heaved himself up and stood beside her.

"Where are we?" Sadie asked.

"Only one way to find out." He put his hand on the glass wall in front of them and, with a cheeky grin, slid it aside.

He jumped down from the high window box. Then he lifted Sadie down slowly, his hands on her waist.

Her bare feet recoiled from the icy stone floor. Its silver insets traced the orbits of planets and stars, forming a celestial map. It was exactly like the ballroom floor in the Star Palace, their most secret hideaway. George had once told her that people believed fate was in the dance of those intertwining paths. So when they danced in their ballroom, their destiny was in the sky above them and below their feet.

But this was not the Star Palace. They'd never been here before.

The long hall had big open doors on both ends. The dioramas stretched to the very ends.

"It's a museum," Sadie said.

"Except we're the ones on display," George said. "Look,

there's Old Charlotte." He pointed to the shell of a smashed truck upside down against a tree. One of the wheels was still spinning.

Sadie turned away from it. The image woke a monster inside her. She could feel it clawing its way out. She couldn't think about it. She didn't dare. She looked toward the end of the hall. There she spotted a big map painted on the wall in the next hallway. Its labyrinthine paths twined like the branches of the Tree of Life.

Sadie heaved a sigh of relief. She loved museums. She was an old hand at sailing through wings and galleries. She consulted the map and figured they were in the "Recent Acquisitions and Highlights" section. A few others jumped out: a portrait hall, a special exhibit on cryptographic technology, and a star in the center of the map that seemed to glow. *The Star Palace,* she thought.

The Star Palace was the end of every adventure, and the site of every climax. It didn't matter if they were playing spies or wizards, if they were detectives or royalty: they always found their way to the palace at the end. That was where happy endings were possible. After a victory, they would dance under a glass ceiling of immutable stars. When the costumes were off and they were no one but themselves, they always took a few moments to enjoy their sanctuary. They would stand on their beautiful balcony and stare out into the lands they had created and remember that no matter how horrible things seemed, all these universes were theirs forever. They were free to confess their greatest fears and admit their greatest sorrows. Not even a diary could offer the safety of the palace.

But it wasn't always easy to get to.

They needed a door, and those only appeared when they had been earned, or when they were needed most. It would take a journey to find it.

One star, glowing. What else could it mean?

She traced the path with her finger. The museum must have been huge.

"Which way should we go?" George asked. Sadie wasn't entirely sure. The paths seemed to bend and twist as she followed them, changing their minds, changing the map.

"Away," she said finally. "To seek and find."

"To seek and find," he replied, slipping his hand into hers.

She turned back to look at the room where they had arrived. A label above the glass read *"Sadie and George: the last adventure?"*

She shuddered. Already the light inside had begun to fade.

✳

They spotted familiar landmarks, each one more and more bewildering. In the Classics hall, they passed the king's bedchambers, where Sadie had once told George one thousand tales to calm his wrath. The whistle of a distant train in the next room called them to a hall filled with a hundred railcars on tracks to nowhere. They'd ridden each of these trains during Sadie's detective novel phase, sharing in the locomotive obsession of their authors. In the cafeteria, they sampled treats from all over the world. Sadie reached into the abandoned buffet to taste treacle tart and tomato sandwiches.

They passed under filigree arches and stained glass windows as they journeyed to the star on the map. It seemed like the more wondrous the surroundings, the farther they were away. Every distraction took them in the wrong direction: George bounded off to admire a statue of himself in all his princely splendor—white coat, white gloves—and the next thing they knew they were twice as far away as they had been. They couldn't help but let the warm silence of the museum wrap them up and comfort them. It was almost as beautiful as the Star Palace itself. Sadie wasn't even angry that they were hopelessly lost. What more could she want? All around her was the story of Sadie and George.

They were somewhere along the outer edge of the building, in a hazy polar dawn Sadie had once dreamed of seeing in the Antarctic winter. The sun would never rise, only threaten light.

"They say the polar winter drives men mad, never seeing the light," George said. He always knew what she was thinking. He always knew her so completely. And he loved her anyway. That was why she could never leave him.

Leave him? Why would I ever have to leave him? she wondered. The truth clawed at her mind.

"Do you remember yet?" he asked as they gazed at the dawn.

"No," she said, though she did, and she knew that he knew it. He would be brave enough to say it for both of them. She knew that just as well.

"You're in a hospital. There was a car crash. If you can't keep our secrets, everyone will know about us," he said. He took her by the shoulders. "Bad things are going to happen."

"What do you mean?"

"If you tell the doctors about me, I'll die."

"George!"

"I believe in you. You can get us out of this. It won't be easy. You'll have to be strong."

"I'm not strong." She covered her face to hide her tears.

"Well, you'll have to be brave, then. You're going to save us."

"How?"

"I don't know. All we have is this. And that's what they want . . . they want your thoughts, your dreams, even your nightmares, even your fears. They want to change you, Sadie. And the worst part is, if they win, you won't even remember. You won't even know. This will feel like a sickness. You won't remember loving me. You won't remember why this is important."

Sadie shuddered. A world without George was worse than anything she could imagine.

In a world without George, she was completely alone.

"I need Occlumency. Like in Harry Potter. I have to close my mind."

"Exactly. Use everything we've learned, every story we've ever lived, to get back to me. I can't be there to help you this time."

"I'm afraid," Sadie said. They stood in the aftershock of her confession for a moment, waiting for it to feel silly and melodramatic, waiting for laughter to come. It all seemed like another story. And yet it wasn't. Not like before.

Music began to play across the museum: a waltz. George held out his hand.

She would find a way back to him. He belonged to her. She knew every stitch of every suit he'd ever worn. His monk strap boots and brogues she'd clipped from stills of James Bond. His face, thin and angular, had washed ashore from the watercolors in her copy of *The Arabian Nights*. And then there were those blue, blue eyes. She could never quite place them on paper or film. But he was hers. Every bit of him, hers.

No one could take that away.

She took his hand and they danced.

"Do you remember when I taught you this?" George asked. Sadie thought. She remembered him teaching her so many times, in so many guises, that she wasn't sure which was the first. She remembered looking it up in a book she'd brought home, with little printed shoes and lines to tell her where her feet should go. She remembered swaying alone in her room with her headphones on, lost in his arms. But their stories lived outside of time, and she could learn again and again with him. Had they ever waltzed before she'd brought home that book? She couldn't remember.

"How is it that *you* taught *me*?" Sadie asked.

"What?"

"How could you teach me if I didn't know it already?" George's eyes darkened, and Sadie was captured in that tumultuous blue sea. But then the waves calmed and he was an ocean of affection again.

"After all this time, how are you surprised by what little magic we have in this world?" he asked, pulling her so close she couldn't breathe. "After all this time, how are you still surprised by the magic of us?"

✳

The beautiful museum faded away as the music dissolved into the whir of machinery. Celestial floors became cold linoleum beneath Sadie's feet.

"It's time for me to go," George said.

"I'll look for you around every corner."

"I won't be there. You have to come to me." He lifted her chin so that she had to look up at him, hypnotized and adrift. "Come find me. You're on your own now."

"I thought we were running away."

"We can't run. This isn't real. But I am. Not in your world, but in ours. I *am* real. Remember that."

"I don't think that's what people mean by real."

"But it exists for us. That's what real is. We *make* this place real for the two of us."

Sadie couldn't argue with that. She'd never felt more real than when she was with George, after all.

"Are you going back to the Star Palace?"

"No, darling." He collapsed onto the bed and put his head in his hands. "I can only go those places with you."

"I thought that was where you lived. That's what you told me." She sat next to him, one hand on his to comfort him.

"I didn't want you to worry. But it's different now. I thought we had more time."

George wrapped the cage of his arms around her.

"So where do you go when you're not with me?"

"Where does music go when you're not playing it? Where does a thought go when you're not thinking it? You've asked yourself those questions over and over because you are afraid to ask what you want to know: what happens to me when I'm not with you?"

"Are you going to tell me?" she asked as bravely as she could, but his focus had snapped to the door, with the intensity he reserved for spy operations, life-and-death situations. Lights were coming on in the hallway, one by one.

Clunk. Clunk. Clunk. The light rushed toward them.

"We're out of time. Just promise me, Sadie, that you'll never let me go. You'll never let me die alone in the dark where no one can find me."

And then he was gone.

30

DAY 2

I wake up completely confused. My parents are here. They're here and they've got luggage and . . . Wait, where is here?

Oh, the hospital. I look around. I look at my leg. I look at my parents.

For a split second, I think I'm free, like this was all a big mistake, and my parents have come and fixed everything like parents are supposed to, and there will be no more talking to Dr. Roberts, who will be very apologetic. And she'll take out some giant official-looking "all better" stamp and just like that I'll be out, STAMP STAMP STAMP, over my folder, and off I'll go, out to the car, and it'll be like none of this ever happened.

Of course. that's not how this works.

My parents flew in insanely early and came straight from the airport, so they actually look worse than I do. They have all their luggage with them from their trip—they were working a car show in Germany, selling the glory of classic

31

American cars to rich German obsessives—and they are delirious from traveling and worrying about me. They left at like two the morning I crashed. They landed, got the phone call, and came back on the next flight.

And they are, needless to say, none too pleased about my accident.

My parents always kind of look like two sides of the same coin, or two halves of a whole. They both have the kind of brown hair that you know was blond when they were babies. They have brown eyes: "Mine are hazel, your *dad's* are brown," my mom always insists, but they're the same color. Worst of all, they are for all practical purposes telepathic. And, like one of those Japanese fighting robots that is made up of smaller robots (like in one of Henry's anime shows), they turn into an unstoppable force when they combine.

Regrettably, that unstoppable force is not seeing things my way at all.

"We're just so glad you're okay," they keep saying, but I'm still half-asleep. Too asleep to even protest the grave injustice happening right before my eyes.

Not only do my parents not insist on taking me home, they actually help wheel me down to what might have at one time been called an asylum but is now called a "psychiatry center." There are no bars, no crazies in straitjackets, just a bunch of way too friendly nurses.

They talk a lot with Dr. Roberts out in the hall. I pretend to busy myself with my notebook so I can eavesdrop more easily.

My dad is saying, "She's never been in trouble, exactly, it's just . . . ," and "Well, it's hard to explain. She's always been . . . ," then a bunch of stuff I can't hear. My mom: "No, she would never . . ." and "What are you saying?" And finally Dr. Roberts says, "I assure you, Mr. and Mrs. Black, it's only a few days," and that I hear completely clearly, almost like she *wants* me to hear her so I know I'm completely screwed.

Traitors. Traitors. Traitors.

But I start to feel ridiculous staring at those words, because of course my parents can't just spring me from this asylum; there's probably some law against that anyway. So I scratch it all out again. But I'm still angry and I don't know why.

My parents finally go home to get cleaned up, and I bury my mortification in sleep.

You know when you fall back asleep and your dreams are more intense? The second time I wake up today, I am in the middle of a dream about wizards and George. Even after my eyes are open I still have one foot in slumberland. I can't help slipping back into my dream: the smell of soot, the long empty platform . . . just like in Harry Potter, the best adventures start with trains.

I've played this scene hundreds of times: George leaning out of the compartment, his arm outstretched to me, his white gloves stained with the blood of our enemies.

"You can make it!" he shouts over the roar of the wind. My fingers brush his hand—

"Sadie. Are you listening? I asked you if someone had been in here with you."

I feel sick as the fingers that belong to George transfigure into a blue latex glove, and my arm that has all the scratches from the crash is not outstretched toward adventure but toward a too-cheery nurse who had been talking in my general direction since she woke me up to apply Muggle medicine over all my scrapes and bruises. Madame Pomfrey she is not.

Dr. Roberts is standing in the doorway talking in my general direction as well.

"No," I say. "I mean, my parents. This nurse."

"Maria," the nurse adds without a glimmer of annoyance.

"Are you sure?" Dr. Roberts asks. "I heard you talking to someone."

This is scary. I've gotten so good at talking with George inside my head that I'm pretty sure no one can tell. But the little cups of painkillers are making me stupid, transparent. Careless. I am leaking secrets everywhere because of whatever I am taking to feel none of this pain. I close the door on pain and open my fantasies to everyone.

"Yeah," I mutter. Monosyllabic communication is usually an excellent strategy for containment. Dr. Roberts keeps at me like a Bond villain.

"Is this yours, then?" Roberts asks. She picks up a red notebook that looks a lot like mine off a chair near the door.

"No," I say, but now she has my attention. "Mine's green." She flips through it, then tucks it into her briefcase.

"Have you seen a girl with hair that's sort of red and blue and yellow? Is she in here?" Roberts is frustrated. Maria just laughs.

"Is she dangerous?" I ask. Her face softens.

"No, not at all. Maybe she's a bit of a trickster. And very good at hiding."

Roberts sizes me up in that clinical way doctors love to pretend makes them smarter than other people. Like they've got a monopoly on observation.

"Sadie, you're very safe here," she assures me.

"We haven't seen her," Maria says, and Roberts turns to leave.

"What's her name?" I call out after her. She turns around, one eyebrow elevated by my sudden interest. She weighs her options and replies:

"She calls herself Eleanor."

⁕

I admit, everything I know about psychiatry is from movies and books and Wikipedia, but I have been pleasantly surprised by the accuracy of my research. It just shows: knowledge is power.

When the appointed hour for cross-examination arrives, Dr. Roberts settles herself into the plastic chair by my door. She likes to sit far away and very still, and I can draw a frame around her and evaluate her all at once.

She waits a long time to say anything, but I certainly am not going to talk first.

Finally, she speaks: "Sadie, I want to continue our conversation from last time. Do you remember what we were talking about?"

"George," I grumble.

Then she gives me one of her long wait-you-out pauses. Beware of silence. It pulls out all your secrets.

While we are waiting, I take some mental notes on her, which I will record later because obviously even though she writes her notes about me right in front of me, I can't exactly do the same.

Dr. Roberts is incredibly pretty. She's black, with straight hair that goes to her shoulders and really big brown eyes. She wears high heels and has a perfect manicure every single day, but her nails are short. She doesn't sound like she's from St. Louis. She sounds like she's from Boston maybe. She is always scribbling and it almost looks like she's doodling. When she is thinking hard about a problem she taps her pen on her lips, which is okay because she doesn't wear lipstick. Her smile is crooked but genuine.

All of that is in the frame, but then there's what's not in the frame too. Like, you wonder: how long does that manicure take? If she's got a Boston accent, where is her family? There's no way she can drive in those shoes, so what shoes did she wear into the office today?

Those are the questions a detective knows to ask. Maybe they help you figure out who the killer is.

"Sadie, let's level," Roberts says.

I win the round of silence, but I've gotten so distracted that I forgot it was even a contest.

"If there's someone out there who's injured, I need to know about it. I'm going to have to ask your parents. Is this someone your parents would know?" she asks.

"No," I say. This is a pin, like in chess. A loss or a loss.

"Your boyfriend, Henry—would he know who George is?" I want to die.

See, I told her about Henry in an attempt to get out of this whole George conversation, and of course it comes back to bite me. In chess it's called an oversight. I'm terrible at chess. Henry might be the only person worse than me. Whenever George and I play, waiting up on a stakeout on one of our Moscow missions, I always lose.

Losing is the most painful part, because you have to watch it happen so slowly. You watch your pieces die on the board in slow motion, watch the death throes of your own cleverness in all its pathetic complexity. In chess you've usually lost the game ten moves back and didn't see it.

Roberts vs. Black was threatening to go this way.

In my head, I recap our previous match.

She asked me straight out: "Did you try to kill yourself?"

I countered: "No, why would I kill myself what with my awesome life and awesome boyfriend named Henry who is totally real and oh also I'm a straight-A student and am in honors English and math and I am a cross-country vice captain and I am so well rounded for serious my life is great." Breathe.

Next move, she went for check: "Did you deliberately hit that tree with your truck?"

I took flight, but I knew right then that I was just racing against checkmate: "Statistically sixteen-year-olds are terrible drivers and I was texting and driving and singing really loud and haven't you ever done something stupid and been really embarrassed and grounded for a really long time?"

But that's how she knows about Henry. You give a little, you get taken to the cleaners.

I try to salvage my position: "No, Henry doesn't know him."

But this move is, again, beyond stupid. *Him* implies that there is a *him* to know. I truly need to get off these painkillers. But my leg hurts a lot.

"So who *does* know George?" she asks, having established the existence of an answer other than "No."

"No one."

"Sadie, we're going to have to be a little more honest with each other—"

"Sadie, you're awake," my mom interrupts, shoving open the door, my dad a step behind. It wasn't locked, of course, but I forgot entirely that it could open. We were in another world, Roberts and I. She turns, as startled as I am. She hops out of her seat.

"Mrs. Black! Mr. Black! We were just—"

"Sorry, are we interrupting?"

"Well, actually—"

"No," I say. Roberts raises an eyebrow at me.

"We'll continue this discussion later," she says. And then she disappears, dissolving into nothing but the sharp click of her heels as she leaves with my unfinished story in her bag.

✳

A shower and some breakfast have calmed my parents way down, but I know they are not happy with me. But the thing is, we don't ever fight anymore. We just let silence and time do the work of forgetting.

My dad busies himself looking at all the TV channels, getting even more disappointed than me as he cycles through them.

"Sucks, right?" I offer.

"Seriously." He turns it off. When I was homeschooled, my dad did most of the schooling part, because Mom was busy with car shows. He was obsessed with staying on track with all these tests, and he could be a real jerk about it because all I wanted to do was read and do literally zero math ever. But sometimes we'd be in a hotel room and Mom would be out and we'd watch hotel movie channels all day and keep it a secret.

I don't mean to say that my parents were my only friends, exactly. I had other homeschooled friends: people I would see at these awkward game nights and book clubs and sports I had to go to so I wouldn't turn out "under-socialized." I had cousins, I had pen pals, I had teammates. I guess those are all friends.

But my parents were my best friends.

And now I can't trust them at all. Not with this.

My mom starts redecorating. She moves the generic vase on the generic dresser and inspects the generic medical equipment. She folds generic blankets and rustles generic blinds. I hate it when people touch my things, but nothing of me is hidden in those places, and so it is safe territory for us both.

Finally, though, I have to speak.

"I'm sorry about the truck," I begin.

"We're just glad you're okay," Mom says. "We brought you some books, some clothes—"

My mom stops when she sees my face. I know I look mortified. It's just that I feel my whole chest seize up when I think of them digging through my room. What could they have found? I think of my closet: a total disaster. I can just picture bits of adventures, completely meaningless to anyone else, tumbling across my floor: a broken cassette case, some white gloves, a map of Russia, textile and wallpaper catalogs, and travel magazines. An old attaché case from the Goodwill, its corners exposed under disintegrating leather. My secret world lying on the floor for anyone to see. If you know how to look, there are universes in that closet.

"We didn't touch anything," Mom assures me. She knows me too well in some ways. She opens the bag and starts putting my stuff out on the nightstand.

"Don't unpack. I'm not going to be here that long."

"Nonsense. We always unpack."

It's a Road Years tradition. Doesn't that sound cool? The Road Years. That's how I think of them, even though we never went that far. Anyway, even if we were only staying the night in nowhere Nebraska, all our suitcases got emptied, and the bathroom shelves got filled. Mom was fast: she could have us set up in ten minutes and strike camp in five, all while my dad was still getting his pants on.

"Anyone been to see you yet?" Dad asks.

"No, I don't think anyone knows I'm here. I couldn't call anyone. I don't have my phone."

"You know Henry's number," he says.

"Yeah, but he's on the road." Right after graduation, Henry got a crazy summer gig subbing for a guitarist on a national tour. He's not even eighteen and he's already a professional. He says it'll pay enough to help fund a real album and maybe a tour for his band, Brother Raja, next year. But it sucks: he's been on the road since June.

I know exactly where he is, down to the latitude and

longitude. I made him a really cool guide to all the places he would see, with maps and local attractions and lots of notes to say I'd miss him. I printed it on my parents' office printers and sewed it all up like a real book.

My parents glance at each other in that meaningful way they always do. They're excellent at talking without saying anything. When they had their radio show, they could be having this whole dynamic conversation on air about the history of Pierce-Arrow hood ornaments and their eyes could be saying, "Did you remember to buy milk?" or "How about spaghetti for dinner?"

I've never been able to crack the code.

"It'd be fun to have your friends visit," my dad says. "I mean . . . Lucie. And Henry."

I try not to look hurt. They don't want me to mess up my tiny little social group. Lucie is the best, the absolute coolest. They can see how even standing near her makes me less invisible. I'm happy to be her sidekick at school.

And Henry . . . My parents might love Henry more than me. He came over once and helped my mom sell one of her old guitars on the Internet, and he spent over an hour explaining Craigslist like he was talking to an alien. Henry said he was happy to do it because he got to be near me.

You don't get to leave a boy like Henry. He's literally perfect.

"Speaking of friends, how's Old Charlotte?" I ask. My parents look aside. "She's totaled, isn't she?"

"Yeah. She just couldn't be salvaged after a second accident," my dad says. Old Charlotte was basically cursed: we'd been driving her when we had our accident five years ago. I sniffle a little bit because deep down I want to believe there isn't a car on the road my parents can't fix. But of course that isn't true.

"We wanted to save Old Charlotte too," Mom says, like wanting something is as good as doing it. "It's okay. We'll talk about getting a new car when you're able to drive it."

"I'm . . . not grounded or anything?"

"Well, no. It was an accident," my dad says, but he says it like a question, or maybe that is in my head.

Then it's like they've run out of lines. They look at each other and I realize I should say something, but what?

The minutes drag on and I know I should be focusing on what is going on. But I am drifting toward George.

And then, because I am thinking about him, I am lost in him. That's the trouble with me and thinking.

"Sadie?" my mom calls softly, nervously, and I remember where I am. I've only been zoned out for a second, but she is staring at me like she's been reading my mind and I feel so exposed and my whole face turns bright red.

"Sorry, I keep . . . fading. It must be the medication. You guys don't have to stay here," I say. "I'm totally fine."

"Don't be ridiculous," Mom says. My dad looks at his shoes. He doesn't like conflict. At the shop, Mom handles all customer-related awfulness, and my dad is responsible for vermin and anything involving scrubbing. They're very happy with this arrangement.

"Well, someone has to keep the shop open. You guys can't hang around here all day."

"Those are called employees," she says with a sass I have clearly inherited. "We can stay."

"Why can't I come home, then? It's just a broken leg."

"It's not *just* a broken leg."

"What, and some staples?"

"Sadie. Come on."

"Yeah, but—"

"Why do you think you're in here? It's because . . ."

"Because they won't believe me!"

"I knew we should have brought you with us, but you wanted to stay and we *trusted you* to be *responsible enough* to do that. You were supposed to be going to Lucie's! What in the world were you doing?"

"I wasn't doing anything! I just went for a drive! This is all a big misunderstanding! Why is everyone trying to turn this into a Lifetime movie?"

My dad raises his eyebrows and my mom replies with hers.

Then my dad does the thing he always did when I was little, where he talks very calmly and it makes me feel like I'm the one being ridiculous even if I'm completely right. He says very soothingly:

"Sadie, we'll be here when you want us to be. The doctors say—"

"I don't care what they say!" I shout.

44

"Okay," he says. "But if you do want us to be here, we're happy to stay."

I settle down. That's what we do. We don't want conflict.

"I don't want to be any trouble."

My parents hang around for an hour or so and we watch TV, like we do at home. We like TV. It's easy to grow apart watching TV, so that's our together time. Together is the biggest lie people tell each other: that being in the same house or in the same room means anything at all. You can be sitting all on the same couch and still be totally alone.

I won't ask them to come back. But at least they brought some of my own clothes, so now I don't have to wear those terrible hospital tie-up things. I felt like I was crawling out of my skin.

Now I have my favorite shirt, which is a Brother Raja T-shirt that Henry gave me. He has the same one, and it feels like holding him. It's the same elephant design that he has on his ring, which does look amazing when he's playing guitar. I have worn this shirt into an almost-nothingness. It is the perfect level of used: it has no holes but barely exists except as an extension of my skin.

I have my things from home. But I'm still alone.

Since I met George, I've never been alone. If I were at home, I would simply let myself go until I dip into that place of enchantment. In the summers I spent days there sometimes when Henry was away. I used to walk all the way to the art museum just to look at things I'd already seen and dream myself to George. I would pack a lunch and leave before dawn if I could, not coming home until after dark. I had beautiful days when I wasn't a part of this world at all.

But without dreams, there's only wakefulness and the blackness of sleep.

✳

I wake up in the night and I feel chilled all the way through my broken leg. My head hurts in that after-nap way, where your body punishes you for having fallen asleep.

My journal is lying open across the bed. I must have dozed off with it in my arms. My words are there for anyone to see.

From what I know of being awake, I prefer to be asleep.

I snatch it up. I can't let it fall into the wrong hands, obviously.

I go to put it in the drawer of the table next to my bed, which I can just barely reach without hurting myself, when I notice a little piece of paper tucked under the edge of the lamp on the table.

I am absolutely sure it was not there before.

I reach and reach for it, stretching every bruised and battered inch of my corporeal form, but it is too far. I move my whole body to the very edge of the bed, nearly crying from the strain, and try again. This time, my fingers brush the torn edges of the paper and, letting out a pathetic groan, I grab it.

I read the words written there.

I put the paper down, my heartbeat like a drumroll announcing my terror.

I look at it again. It is real.

I inspect the note. It is a crookedly torn piece of paper with blue lines, just like the pages out of my notebook. I line up the lines with a page from my journal to make sure: an exact match. Did someone rip this page out of my notebook while I was asleep? I can't find any torn page to match the edges on the note, just my own redactions I've thoroughly torn to bits. But it could have been done while I was sleeping, and the page might have been torn cleanly and ripped later.

One thing is clear: someone has been in my room.

I look at the note again, trying to see clues. The handwriting is desperate, scribbled.

Watch out.
They will steal your dreams.
Your Friend Eleanor

THE NOBLE AND MOST
ANCIENT HOUSE OF BLACK

"Damn," George muttered. They were sunk low against the wall under the window. The heavy velvet curtains, once capable of turning noon to night, had been mutilated into lace. The lovely floral wallpaper had blossomed with bullet holes. The charming string quartet waltzes of the night before had been replaced by gunshots and screaming, marching orders and sirens. It had been such a nice hotel room. Such a shame.

George's tie was a crumpled knot and his white shirt was stained with blood. He kicked open his attaché case and pulled out his cigarettes, lighting two and handing one to Sadie. She took a drag and peeked out the window over her shoulder.

The police cars below were no problem—their real concern was the Agency. Sadie could hear the small fleet of assassins on the stairs, the clumsy fools. Feet of lead, brains of toxic sludge, armed to the teeth with dirty weapons. They would think nothing of blowing up the building and half the block with it just to end two agents of the Resistance.

"We're surrounded," Sadie concluded. She reached into her holster and pulled out her last bullets: two bright coppery monuments to death looming large in her small hand. She considered the bullets like the scientist she still was. They were simple. Efficient. The idea of dying next to George didn't seem so terrible, if one had to die. And one way or another, it seemed rather less than optional. At best she might choose the bullet. After all, there were only two rules in the Resistance: do good, and don't be taken alive.

George glanced over. He was making the same calculations.

Destiny had plucked her out of the lab, out of the top of her class at MIT, and into this network of betrayal and deceit: the war under the surface of every country, every city, every street. And George hadn't even wanted her. Not at first. "Don't send a physicist to do a spy's job!" he had shouted. "Be patient with him," Control had told her. "He's young, but he's the best."

How things had changed. That night at the Metropol after she'd saved his life, the way he had looked at her. Those deep blue eyes: a boy of loneliness and mystery. She studied him now, and she knew he wasn't afraid to die. And after accomplishing so much, after *living* so much, neither was she. She wouldn't have traded it for a hundred years in a lab.

Falling stars. That's what they were: burning bright and over too soon. But they'd been stars. What more could two people ask for in this crazy world?

George glanced sideways at the gun in Sadie's hand as another bullet shattered the chandelier. He slowly blew a ring of smoke and watched it float toward the ceiling. The door cracked and splintered as the agents outside worked to break it down.

He reached out without a word and took the pistol from her. She barely felt the gun leave her hand. Sadie took one last drag and put out the cigarette. She handed him the bullets.

"We might still make it out," George offered feebly. She heard the barest hint of weakness, that vulnerable spot that only she knew. He conducted some legerdemain of bullets and chamber. His fingers barely trembled.

"You know we can't risk it," Sadie said. He reached out and grabbed her, holding her tight.

"I love you," George said, the muzzle of the gun pressed into her hair. She closed her eyes. The world went silent as they retreated into this final still frame. They wanted to want something else, but they knew that this, here, was perfect.

"I know," Sadie replied.

BANG.

*

BANG BANG BANG.

"Sadie, get up," her mom shouted, knocking on the door. "You'll be late for practice."

"I am up," Sadie shouted back. "I just had my head-phones on."

For her thirteenth birthday present to herself from George, she'd installed a lock on her bedroom door. It had been easier than she'd thought: all those homeschool shop classes playing with hammers and screwdrivers had been worth something after all. It had been a new world of bliss-ful locked safety. Her parents had tried reasoning with her, and had shared several eyeball conversations over this matter, and she presumed many more behind closed doors. Now there was an extra key in the kitchen. But they always did prize inventiveness, and the lock stayed.

Sadie opened the door. Her mom's fist was poised for another *BANG.* She was wearing a T-shirt for Webster Groves High School, one from when she'd gone there her-self. Orange and black were unflattering on everyone, but especially did no favors in her family.

Middle school hadn't been over two days, and already she had to go to cross-country practices for the high school team.

"I'll be up in a minute."

"We're so excited! Dad made you breakfast! First prac-tice for our big high school girl!"

"You know they let everyone on the team, right? Like,

51

it's not even a team. It's literally running in circles like a hamster."

"Hamsters run on wheels."

"Or like aquarium fish. Who can't remember where they started."

"That makes even less sense. Work on your analogies before you surface. Homeschoolers are supposed to be better on verbal tests."

"I'm not homeschooled anymore, though. Those are public middle school analogies. Sadie is to cross-country run as fish is to tank circuit."

"Oh, stop being such a spoilsport. You love school. And you'll love cross-country. Remember all those 10Ks we used to do? It's just like that."

Sadie glanced at the floor. Her laundry was full of shirts from those races. She'd almost grown out of them, but she had them in every possible color, for every possible cause and holiday. When she'd been younger it seemed like there was one every other week. Her parents had a whole matching set, but they couldn't really run anymore. Theirs had become oily auto shop rags.

Sadie watched as her mom hobbled back up the stairs. Before the crash, she would have raced up from the basement.

Sadie shut herself in her bedroom and got dressed. All around her house were little reminders of the life that had been ripped out from under them: her parents' crooked walks, the way they drove so carefully, Old Charlotte herself. Everything around her brought back memories that tingled at the edges of her mind. She felt like the only person in her house who could see memories in every magnet and mug. To her parents, walking by these things every day made them invisible. Sadie couldn't help but see. She shook the thoughts away.

And her mom was wrong: Sadie didn't love school. She'd never been lonelier in her whole life.

"Well, not with me around," said George.

Sadie smiled. That much was true.

✳

The track wasn't far, but her parents insisted on dropping her off, and in one of the flashier cars they were working on. They waved like mad people as they sputtered off in a semi-functional Model T. Everyone stared.

Sadie used to like it when everyone admired their cars. Her parents were always happy to talk shop with any interested passersby. They'd hand out cards, advertise their services. But that had been before the crash, when she hadn't had to go to school. Since middle school, everyone her parents talked to might be someone else's mom or dad. It wasn't like they were far away in Kentucky, Ohio, Nevada, anymore. They weren't strangers here in St. Louis, they were neighbors.

But she had to admit, it was still a pretty cool car.

Not knowing exactly what to do, Sadie followed the

spotty trail of girls down to the track. She could see twenty or so other kids—some just out of middle school, lots of high schoolers—sitting on the grass. She didn't see anyone she'd had a class with, and she hadn't expected to see any friends . . . even after two years, she didn't really have any.

She followed their example and sat down on the grass. More kids kept arriving until it seemed like there was no way all of them would fit on a single team. They looked more like a herd. Cross-country was the sport they asked you to do if you weren't interested in anything else. It was okay to just show up to practice, and it got you out of gym class. That was the only reason she hadn't put up a bigger fight: if she stayed quiet and trotted along behind the other girls, no one would bother her, and she wouldn't have to face gym next year.

Sadie spotted another girl who looked like she was new too. She was wearing a Quidditch T-shirt and bright orange running shorts. She was black and thin, and had bright blue nail polish. She had cool blue streaks in her hair, which she was busily putting into a puffy ponytail. Sadie rearranged her own ponytail and then performed what she hoped was an acceptable imitation of stretching.

A woman was walking around getting their names on a clipboard. She stopped in front of the girl.

"Lucille Washington?" she asked.

"Lucie," the girl corrected her. "Please don't call me Lucille," she said quietly.

The woman smiled. She seemed nice.

She turned to the group.

"Okay, we're going to start with introductions. I am Mrs. Vaughn, and I teach history at the high school. For those of you who are returning, you know the drill. We're just going to get to know each other and take a jog around the neighborhood today, but for the rest of the summer, you're going to train like warriors. We've got a strong group of young women here, and . . ."

She kept talking, but Sadie couldn't follow what she was saying. It sounded awful. There was a lot of talk of endurance and race speeds and percentages, as well as push-ups and gym time. This did not sound fun in the slightest. And what in the world was a fartlek run?

". . . and in our annual tradition," said Mrs. Vaughn, "we will have our puppy run next week before it gets too hot."

"Puppy run?" asked Lucie. The younger girls looked at her. They didn't know they were allowed to talk.

"It's exactly what it sounds like," explained an older girl. "We take a bunch of shelter dogs on a run around the neighborhood."

"Oh. My. God. I *love* dogs," said Lucie.

"Well, great. Something to look forward to," said Mrs. Vaughn. "Now we'll go around and introduce ourselves. Do you want to start, Lucie?"

"Sure!" She stood up and put her hands on her hips like Peter Pan. "Uh . . . what do I say?"

"How about your name, your grade, and something you like."

"Cool. My name is Lucie Washington and I am going to be a ninth grader but I didn't go to middle school here because I just moved from New Orleans and I love Harry Potter." She pointed emphatically to her shirt. She sat down, but then sprang back up again. "Oh, and I love dogs. And running."

Then she sat down again. The older girls were laughing. Sadie couldn't tell if they were laughing at her or with her. Her heart pounded, knowing her turn would come.

"That's great," said Mrs. Vaughn. "How about you, Captain?"

One of the older girls said: "Fine, but I'm not standing, Mrs. V. You're not actually our commander."

"That's right. *You* are." Mrs. Vaughn saluted, and all the girls laughed.

The other girls introduced themselves—they liked everything from anime to volunteering at the zoo—and eventually they wound their way to the back, where Sadie and a few other shy girls were sitting. Sadie mumbled into her shirt: "My name is Sadie—"

"Louder, Sadie!" shouted Mrs. Vaughn.

Sadie spoke up, but then she was too loud: "MY NAME IS SADIE AND I AM IN NINTH GRADE AND I LIKE..."

She paused.

"Yes?" asked Mrs. Vaughn.

"Reading," Sadie said finally.

Her face was bright red. Why couldn't she just say something clever for once in her life? She couldn't come up with anything better? Of course not. All the things she really liked were done with George. Why couldn't she be just reasonably acceptable as a human being for once in her life?

Once the introductions were over, Mrs. Vaughn clapped her hands and, led by the older girls, the whole group set off on a path they all seemed to know already. Sadie was still lost in the spiral of her embarrassment.

"Sadie? Right?"

Sadie looked up and Mrs. Vaughn was standing over her. The other girls were already almost off the field. Sadie nodded.

"Where are you supposed to be?"

"Uhhhhhhhh . . ."

"Uuuuuup and running," Mrs. Vaughn said. "Go on!"

Sadie charged after the other girls, because she didn't want to get lost. She made her way to the mix of girls in the back of the pack. They'd spread out, naturally. Two of the veterans ran back and forth, encouraging them along like sheepdogs. Some of the new girls were chatting, but mostly they stayed a few feet apart, painfully trudging on.

Sadie's feet hurt because her dad had bought her brand-new shoes for the occasion. Her legs were sticky. She had sweat in her eyes.

How long is this run supposed to be? she thought.

"Just to the edge of the forest," answered George. He pulled out his wand and cast a spell behind them. "We'll be safe there."

"It's never safe," Sadie replied, the houses becoming thick, old-growth forest. Her robes surrounded her and magic took over.

✳

The trees were insufficient cover, even with George's protection spells. Sadie could still hear the dragon above as they raced through the forest, jumping over the huge roots of trees. Its great wings brushed the treetops as it searched for the stone they had stolen.

"What is it?" Sadie asked breathlessly, holding the gemstone in her hand. They'd fought demons, ridden wolves, and run. Oh God, had they run.

"A soul," George wheezed, out of breath himself. "Trapped in a stone." The dragon above screamed, and they changed directions just in time to avoid the fireball meant for them.

"How did that happen?"

"Sadie, is now really the time?" He vaulted a felled tree, glancing up into the canopy.

"If I'm going to die for something you insisted we steal, I want to know what it is!"

George groaned. He didn't stop, but he raised his wand and fired away into the heavens, trying to distract the furious beast.

"Sometimes," he said breathlessly, "when a witch or a

wizard is broken by an especially powerful spell, their soul splits up into pieces like jewels. This one is only one part of that soul. Their body may still be wandering around out there, empty."

"What do we do with it?"

"Keep it safe. There's nothing we can do to help right now."

Sadie held it to her ear as she zigzagged through the fallen trees. She thought she could hear screaming coming from inside.

"Can't we set the soul free?"

"No," George said sharply. "That would kill the person inside, whoever they are."

"It must feel so alone," Sadie said.

"We'll have to find a way to put whoever this is back together," George said. "But even if they're alone, they're safe in there. Just be careful with that stone."

The dragon screamed. Sadie lurched forward, almost dropping the jewel. She snatched it out of the air as she fell into step. The forest vanished, and she was off balance but still running.

Oh my God, she thought. *How long have I been with George?*

She was in the neighborhood near the high school. She had no clue how far they'd run.

"Okay, Sadie?" asked one of the older girls.

"Yeah, just tripped," she managed to reply. She couldn't

remember any of the other girls' names. She hadn't been paying attention. As usual.

As they rounded the corner, Sadie realized that all the other girls she recognized from school were well behind her. She was surrounded by lean, focused high schoolers. How had that happened?

She slowed her stride, falling a little back. She didn't want to bother the older girls. She hadn't realized how hard she'd been running. Her head had started to hurt.

As soon as she'd fallen a few paces back, she heard panting next to her. It was Lucie. She looked mad. She was running as hard as she could and her face showed it. She was fast, but she couldn't catch up. All the new girls were tired. Lucie would sprint, then slow, charge, then slow. Sadie ran ahead of her, trying to stay out of her way. Lucie sped up. She couldn't pass Sadie, but she was able to run right next to her. Sadie didn't know what to do, so she just kept running.

As they charged back toward the track, Lucie pulled a little ahead. Seeing the goal seemed to fill her with energy. When Lucie sped up, it was easy for Sadie to speed up with her. It was like they were in sync.

They ran faster and faster and faster until they were both sprinting as hard as they could. Sadie could hear the older girls cheering. The unspoken goal line—Mrs. Vaughn— was yards, then feet, away.

They crossed it at exactly the same moment.

✳

They both collapsed onto the grass. Sadie was too tired to think of anything but the green grass beneath her in strange, sharp focus. Her heart was pounding. *Heatstroke,* she thought.

"Well done, ladies," said Mrs. Vaughn. "But it's a good idea to pace yourself too."

"Who won?" Lucie demanded, so winded she could barely speak.

"No one won. It's not a race," said Mrs. Vaughn. "Remember, we're not running against each other. We're running *with* each other. We're a team."

"You can't run as a team. You're not passing a ball or anything," Lucie gasped out. Sadie nodded.

"Well, everyone runs their own race, but we are stronger when we run that race together."

Lucie suddenly stood, shaky-kneed, and threw up.

"Agreed," said Sadie.

Lucie fell back onto the grass and laughed and laughed.

DAY 3

I'm sitting in a hospital bed, basically unable to move, but my heart is pounding like that feeling I get right before we have a race. It's not a good or a bad feeling. It's a combination of excitement and dread.

Lucie is coming. So is Mrs. Vaughn.

I can feel the moments ticking by. I used to feel that too on race day: the extreme strangeness of moments that are here and then gone. I get so nervous waiting for things to happen. When I'm alone and in my head, it's almost unbearable.

But not on race days anymore, because a team of girls who have spent all morning making French braids and eating peanut butter and spoiling Lucie's foster dogs could drown out any introspection. Mostly I like to be alone, but sometimes it's nice to be on a team.

Team is such a funny word in cross-country. It's not really a team sport, not like soccer or baseball. Mrs. Vaughn's motto, "Everyone runs their own race, but we are stronger when we run that race together," is such a bad motto that we all make fun of it every year. We even put it on our T-shirts ironically, which is fine because Mrs. Vaughn is in on the joke. One time she told me: "Yep. It's super-corny. But the reason you guys love to hate it so much is because you know it's true."

Our cross-country team is a weird cross section of people who weren't good at anything but have to play a sport and real athletes who play a spring sport and need something to do in the fall. That's my best friend, Lucie. She's a soccer star all spring. And then there are people like me who are not even slightly interested but who are awfully fast anyway. It's totally different than real sports because no one gets cut.

We do a few cool things as a team. Pizza parties. Sleepovers. Running, of course. Every summer we take a bunch of shelter dogs on a run. I didn't really like it at first: the summer before freshman year, the summer I met Lucie, I tried to fake sick but my parents made me go. I ran with a dog who kept trying to bite me. I've had bad luck on our annual puppy runs. Lucie loves it, though. Her parents have let her foster every dog she's run with. We like to dress up her dogs as superheroes and take pictures of them and make Twitter accounts for them so they can talk to one another even after they get adopted. She has a house full of pets because she has to take home every stray she touches, if only to make sure that it finds its forever home.

It's kind of what makes her a good friend and a good leader: she doesn't need a reason to like you, she just likes you out of the box. She's a good person. She thinks everyone she meets is a good person too. Even me.

I don't want Lucie to see me like this.

I don't want anyone to see me like this.

I close my notebook at five minutes to nine. I've been dreading this. But it's here now. Time marches forward even if you wish it would stop.

As predicted, Lucie and Mrs. Vaughn are outside my door the split second visitors are allowed. Mrs. Vaughn asks a lot of technical questions about my summer reading, which I definitely intend to complete, and Lucie tells me all about the practices I'm missing.

It becomes clear that none of us are going to talk about the fact that I'm in a hospital. Mrs. Vaughn is sporting her worried parent look, and Lucie is cool enough to know what you do and do not say in mixed company. We are at a standoff: Mrs. Vaughn won't ask parent-y questions in front of Lucie, and Lucie won't ask friend questions in front of Mrs. Vaughn. Result: awkward, stilted silence.

"I bet this will cheer you up. Henry sent you a present," Lucie says. She withdraws a small box wrapped in blue paper with Scotch tape coming undone on all sides. A classic Lucie job. She plays bass, which is good for her "gross club fingers," as she calls them.

I rip the paper right in front of them. I'm usually much

more *secretive*—that's my family's favorite word—but I want to know. I want to somehow find out what Henry knows . . . if he knows about George. I love Henry more than any other real person alive. He's the only real person I've ever been in love with. If he ever finds out about George, it will kill him, and that will kill me.

It's a little blue iPod shuffle. The clippy kind.

"Since I had to put the songs he picked on it and I had to wrap it, it's basically from both of us," Lucie says. "Unless you don't like it. In which case it is strictly from Henry."

"I love it," I say.

With a boy like Henry, the ultimate show of trust is plugging your phone into the speakers on random. I only have cool music on my phone. He'd never say it, but someday he'll see me for what I really am, and he'll realize that he doesn't love me, he just feels obligated.

"Can you tell him thank you?" I ask, cradling the little iPod in my hands like a broken robin's egg.

"He'll be home in a few days. You can tell him yourself," Lucie says. I must look mortified because she continues: "You look totally fine. Really. Maybe you could call him. He's been trying to reach you. He's been texting me like crazy."

She flashes her phone at me. I can't read it that quickly, but I see my name over and over on the screen.

"I don't have a phone," I tell her, but I know he's been calling the hospital. The nurses say, "There's a young beau calling for Miss Sadie," and I always say I'm asleep and I'll call back later. I'm afraid to talk to him. I can't give anything away. He's too good a guesser.

Like this: I love mixtapes. I've never told Henry. But he knows because he watches. It's the difference between someone who can remember facts about you and someone who is in tune with you.

When I was little, my parents made a mixtape for road trips on a real cassette tape. We would be in the car for ages, and I made them play it so many times that it didn't even have a title, it was just The Tape. When they would get tired of it and turn it off, I would get so mad. I threw epic temper tantrums. I never get mad like that anymore. I just fade to black.

It was a Beatles mix because back in the day, my mom was a Beatles superfan proto-fangirl, pre-Internet style. I kind of think my dad slipped in on a vague resemblance to Ringo Starr and a Polaroid of him holding two drumsticks midbeat in his high school band. (I've seen it. He looks one hundred percent as lame as you are picturing.) He liked the Beatles too, and that's how Mom and Dad got into doing these local radio shows about cars and music. They're such nerds. You should hear my parents talk about the merits of two basically identical Mustangs, or make a top-ten Beatles list.

I always count myself extremely lucky that Dad's rational, mechanical approach to life nixed such baby names as Prudence and Jojo. That's right: Mom almost named me Prudence, and I would never have forgiven her, and Dad will still never let her live it down. Sadie was a compromise. Though honestly, I think Sadie is pretty much unacceptable. Sadie is a good name for an obedient golden retriever.

Sometimes I like to imagine what my life would have been like as a Lucy. That's my favorite Beatles name. And yes, my best friend's name is Lucie. No one would ever call her Lucille. But Sadie doesn't shorten to anything good.

Lucy is such a cool name. I can imagine who Lucy Black would have been so easily. Lucy's hobby is horseback archery. Lucy paints detailed portraits of Humane Society dogs. Lucy is in calculus this year instead of precalc, and plays electric violin.

If Lucy were lying here, she'd be dying. She'd be a shark bite victim or maybe have been wounded pulling a stranger out of a burning car about to explode. Something cool. She wouldn't have a broken leg.

For better or worse, I am just Sadie. I think a name says a lot about you. Your name is kind of like your destiny—people make all kinds of guesses about you because of your name. Doesn't that seem too much like fate?

Anyway, I don't really listen to the Beatles anymore. The Tape, the one I loved so much, was falling apart, and the sound had deteriorated, but it was still my favorite until I lost it: it got eaten by Old Charlotte the summer before ninth grade. It survived a car crash, but it couldn't escape its fate. That pretty much ended the Beatles for me. My parents listen to NPR now. I don't know about at work, but they don't listen to rock and roll at home. I miss that tape sometimes. Every single song was magic. I listened to it so many times that it felt like my own thoughts.

Lucie coughs loudly, and I remember where I am. The room pulls into focus and my thoughts recede. Mrs. Vaughn is looking at me, very concerned.

"I'll call as soon as I have a phone," I say, and Lucie starts texting Henry. This is so awkward. "Thanks for visiting," I tell Mrs. Vaughn. She nods, but that uniquely annoying look of parental concern does not leave her face.

"I'm going to go chat with your parents. It's good to see you, Sadie. Lucie, come find me when you're ready."

She leaves us and Lucie laughs, snapping her fingers in front of my eyes to wake me up.

"God, sometimes I think you're secretly a stoner, you're so moony," she says. She jumps up and starts rummaging through my stuff. Lucie and I never hang out in my room because she cannot help but rummage everywhere she goes. My room is a disaster of dreams, and she finds clues too easily.

Lucie's room is military-spotless exactly once a week when her mom checks it, and then it's like a bomb made of sports bras and video games and Quidditch and bass guitar exploded right on her bed. She's been the bass player for Henry's band, Brother Raja, since the very beginning, and so we usually hang out at her place before they practice, or after we go running. I find her stories all over her room. She loves to tell those stories, one for every clue I find. I know I have too many secrets to let her find mine.

"So," she starts, "like . . . you know this is a psych ward, right?"

"Yeah," I say. But she doesn't look embarrassed. She's super-excited.

"So cool. So, so cool."

"It's really not. I mean, it's just a mandatory hold. It's not like I'm supposed to be here or anything."

"Oh, I get it. But still. It's so cool. It's like we're behind the scenes in a scary movie. What do you do here?"

"Uh . . . color. Watch TV. Read. Talk. That kind of thing."

"So basically what you do at home."

Lucie is always talking, always moving. She's always working on a project or running from practice to practice. I can see that being trapped like I am would drive her crazy.

I like to hang out with her between all her missions because there's always something to help with: a poster that needs painting, or a guitar that needs stringing, or some drama with her other friends she wants to vent about. Sometimes I listen to her try out songs, and it makes me happy that she cares what I think. She makes me feel useful. I'm a good sidekick.

"What are you working on?" She points to my notebook.

"Oh. I'm supposed to be writing a story. There's a lot of kindergarten tasks here."

"What kind of story?"

"I don't know. A 'true' story, whatever that means."

I really *don't* know what that means. It's one of the tasks

Roberts has extracted from me in order to secure my release. She asked me to write "one true story."

"What if I can't tell the truth?" I asked her.

"You'll find a way. There are a lot of ways to tell the truth."

I probably rolled my eyes.

"You love going to museums, right? You like art?" I shrugged. I like museums: walking around and stepping through frames to other worlds. Art is somewhat incidental to my liking of it.

My indifference took some of the "cool doctor" wind out of her sails, but she plowed ahead anyway. She pulled out her phone and swiped through some pictures. Then she showed one to me. It was Van Gogh's last self-portrait: the swirly one. I think his eyes are so beautiful and sad. Supposedly his final words were "The sadness will last forever."

"So what do you think? Is this true?" Roberts asked. I shrugged, and she took back her phone.

"You might say it's not realistic, but it's true," she said. "How about this?"

She flashed what I could only assume was a big Pantone swatch of Rothko at me.

"I dunno. I guess if you like that kind of thing."

"Rothko was trying to tell a big truth, in his way. He was obsessed with truth. The point is, you can tell the truth in a lot of ways. I want you to tell the truth however you see fit."

This, to me, seems like a lot of ridiculous art therapy

bullshit on the level of teaching angry girls to ride horses, but I nodded because I wanted her to go away.

"I won't read it if you don't want to show it to me," Roberts said sweetly. "But I think seeing it yourself would be good. So try to find it. The truth."

I really, really dislike this project.

Lucie is staring at my notebook because I zoned out again and I happen to be staring at it too. This time, she looks a little annoyed.

"Where are you?" she asks me.

"Huh? Oh. Sorry. You know, I am basically a stoner right now," I say. "Pain drugs. So high."

She laughs at that, and for the moment, at least, my mask is firmly in place.

And I know she wants to read my notebook, but she won't ask. People hold back all kinds of things you know they would ask you if they could.

"Oh man. Well, I'll write some new fan fiction in solidarity," she says finally. "Can you get online?"

"No. I don't even have a phone."

"Seriously?"

"Yeah. I'll be home in a few days, though."

"Cool. But I guess you're not going to be running anytime soon."

I look pointedly at my leg.

"Sucks. Senior year and everything. Who will be my cocaptain?"

"Vice captain," I correct her.

"*Co*," she insists. Technically, I was voted vice captain. But Lucie wasn't having it.

"Well, it's not like I was any good at it."

"None of us are any good at it," Lucie says. "But the team misses you. Everyone wanted to know if they could come see you, but I said no. I thought you wouldn't like that." I doubt anyone but Lucie even cared about seeing me. They probably just felt obligated.

"Well, it was cool of you to come," I say. "I appreciate it."

"I *appreciate* it," she mimics. "God, you're like a middle-aged businessman sometimes. You sound like my dad."

"Well, I do," I say quietly, and she gives me a gigantic Lucie hug, which is like no other hug ever because it is too tight, and very lopsided. It's the perfect hug. "I really do."

✳

I pick up my new iPod, but I don't want to hear the sounds of Henry. I hide it in a drawer, out of sight.

I open up a Harry Potter book and start half-reading. I know that story so well, my eyes just dance across the pages, the words conjuring the places I've been a thousand times before.

I visit all my old haunts: the Hogwarts library, the Three Broomsticks, Flourish and Blotts. I try to fill in the space all around me with that other world. I try to pave the linoleum with cobblestones and brick myself in with magic. I want to feel George's hand taking mine, the way he does when he sneaks up on me and suddenly we're off on an adventure. But it isn't to be.

I read but the words stay on the page, and I am in a hospital room and my hands are holding a book and I am alone.

You want the truth? The truth is that I'm all alone.

It is on this self-pitying observation that I notice the pixie standing in my doorway. I know who she is immediately. She has foreshadowed herself, written her hints into my story.

Maybe "pixie" is not the best way to describe her. She is a Titan: she dominates every breath I take from the instant I see her.

She is wearing a shark costume, and her arms are crossed and wrapped with pink bandages, her hospital bracelet nestled among a few long strands of technicolor pony beads. Her crazy hair is dyed all sorts of colors, but it has grown way out so that it looks like she has a white-blond crown on top.

"Hi," she says. "My name is Eleanor."

THE BURROW

Mr. and Mrs. Black began their morning in precisely the same manner each and every day. It could be tracked in doors closing, in kettles whistling, in the elevator jazz intro to *Morning Edition* on NPR. At thirteen, Sadie knew this soundtrack so well she could watch the movie of their morning from under her covers in bed. She no longer hovered at the kitchen table observing the clockwork staging of coffee, breakfast, and morning news. She pretended to sleep late—a privilege of having just graduated eighth grade—and the machinery of the household turned without her.

When the Foley track above went silent, Sadie peered out from under the covers. It was perpetually night in the windowless basement, and her phone-turned-flashlight glowed over the disarray of her bedroom until it passed over a pair of black shoes with one toe impatiently tapping away.

George sprang to life, flipping on the lights and tossing her a pair of cutoffs and her Ravenclaw T-shirt, which was almost too small. She recoiled from the fluorescent assault, covering her eyes. "Welcome to summer. Eighth grade—done! No school, no cross-country practice today, nothing but you and me!" he shouted.

"Good morning to you too," she said, blinking. George rifled through her closet as she got dressed, tossing out maps, disguises, wands, potions, keys, and books. He had to dig quite far to find what he was looking for: her spy notebook and fedora. He held them up expectantly.

"Breakfast, George."

He let out an elaborate sigh.

"Come on, then."

They raced up the stairs from the basement into the empty house, their feet beating the carpeted steps as one.

"What do you want to do today?" Sadie asked. She glanced at the itinerary her parents had left her stuck under her lunch box: the plan she'd agreed to the night before. Everything she was going to do was already written down: breakfast, library, clean her room, dinner at seven. She wasn't really free with her day scheduled down to the minute. She texted her parents that she was awake and having breakfast. Then she crossed "eat breakfast" off the list.

She was always being told she needed "structure." The only place she was ever free was in her head.

George handed her a giant bag of store-brand Froot Loops to distract her. It was mostly empty and disintegrating. She poured a rainbow of rings and fairy dust into her bowl, doused it with too much milk, and carried it as cautiously as a circus performer to the living room.

"We could go to Moscow."

"We're going to the library." It was on the itinerary.

"I know why you want to go there," George teased. Sadie's cereal balancing act tottered, but she recovered.

"We'll also go to Moscow. It's a long walk."

"Good."

Sadie sat carefully down on the couch, where she was Forbidden to Eat Anything on Pain of Death or, Worse, Confiscated Phone, as established in the bylaws set out by her mom. George vaulted the back of the couch and landed with a thump next to her, causing a tidal wave of milk to spill over her bowl. Sadie shot him a glare. He grinned sheepishly and turned on the TV. The tail end of *Casablanca* was playing, and Humphrey Bogart was putting Ingrid Bergman on the plane.

"'If that plane leaves the ground and you're not with him, you'll regret it. Maybe not today. Maybe not tomorrow, but soon and for the rest of your life,'" George recited along with the TV.

Sadie tried to reply, but her mouth was full of cereal. George laughed and then she laughed and then cereal was everywhere.

It was the best way to start a summer day all alone.

✳

Every summer day she could, Sadie walked to the library. She walked along precisely the same route, listening to exactly the same music. She knew every house and every tree, every crack in every sidewalk. By noon it would be too hot, so her routine began just after the morning movie on TV.

The weather and her long fantasies during these walks were the only elements that varied. Sometimes the movie she'd watched would creep into her mind, and she and George would be off swashbuckling, solving murders, or performing elaborate tap numbers. Sometimes she imagined her life as it might have been: running away with George, hopping a train to L.A. to become an actress, or conning her way onto a plane to become an Australian citizen, living free in the outback. She had been working on her accent since elementary school. When she arrived at the library, whatever she had dreamed up needed details, research. She pulled real paper encyclopedias out of the dusty land of exile in the back of the building. She dug up atlases and pored over travel books. And by midafternoon, she'd be settled in at a huge table with a novel in her lap and half the world laid out before her.

George didn't sit with her in the library. Why would he, when there were pages and pages to explore? She followed him down into the depths of the catacombs of Paris, and to the top of the world's highest mountains. She sat alone, though she was never truly alone. After all, she wasn't really there.

So it came as a great surprise when, last summer, an intruder sat down across from her with a book, tethering her solidly in the library and distracting her with reality, much to George's displeasure.

He was a little older than she was, with dark hair and brown eyes. He wore T-shirts of bands Sadie had never heard of. (Surreptitiously, she Googled them on her phone.) He read manga and Lord of the Rings and sometimes a music theory textbook feathered with sticky notes. He sat on a diagonal from her, with his legs stretched under the table to rest his dirty Converse high-tops on the chair next to hers. His legs barely made it. He had to slouch low, nearly sliding off the chair. It was as though he wanted her to see his shoes. Even when she looked down, he was in her peripheral vision.

All this Sadie observed with the precision of a spy. It drove George crazy. She couldn't quite get away with the dark-haired boy around.

She knew that she had read too much into his choice of seats. It was a big table, after all. Maybe he was only sitting with her because he felt bad for her, all alone. Maybe he didn't even realize he was sitting *with* her at all, so much as near her.

She'd seen him around town, but she'd ducked away. He wasn't at her school, that was for sure. She didn't know his name. Today, she wondered what he would read this summer, when she dared to imagine that he'd be there.

George coughed next to her. He was jealous of her treacherous thoughts. He'd been shut out, fading away.

"Are you going to be like this all summer?" he asked

as she locked the front door. She shifted her backpack on her shoulder. George's attaché case had all the important things, of course: ransom money, their guns, the keys to the Aston Martin. But the necessities of reality were heavy in her backpack. She had books to return, water to carry, a lunch box her mom had left her, house keys, phone. George never seemed burdened.

Once he had her attention, he bolted ahead, around the house to the backyard, to Old Charlotte. She chased him, sprinting, her heart pounding. As soon as she started running, her problems faded away. They always did. Laughing, she hopped into Old Charlotte and reached under the seat for The Tape. Even touching it sent relief coursing through her veins.

Most of the time, worries caroled across her mind, chanting and singing like a choir, their voices amplified as though in a perfect cathedral. She couldn't escape the music in her mind, but she could replace it. When the Fab Four, as her mom called them, took their places on the stage in her head, there was no room for other voices. They silenced the real world and drew her into another one.

George readied himself as she closed the truck door. She slipped in her earbuds and her feet started their automatic march toward the library. The Beatles began to sing, and Sadie and George were back in the thick of a mission they'd paused, out of breath and on the run. The sun began to rise on Tverskaya Street in Moscow, footsteps echoed behind her, and the suburbs were gone.

When they reached the library, it was as though no time had passed since they'd left home. Daydreams were like that. Lifetimes passed in no time. But a bolt of disappointment shot through her and blew George away as she resurfaced: a lanky teenage boy stood staring at a white sign on the library door. Sadie could see that it said CLOSED in giant red Sharpie letters.

She turned away, trying not to cry from disappointment. There was always tomorrow. But she fell down a spiral of disorientation: she'd been so excited for the library, and now she'd have to go home, and—

"Hey!" shouted the boy behind her. She turned, red-eyed.

It was him. He had grown half a foot since she'd seen him last. He wore his hair longer and his face was mottled with acne, but his eyes were the same. Big brown doe eyes, perfect and kind.

"It's closed?" Sadie asked, staring at the handwritten sign.

"The air-conditioning broke down." They stood in silence shoulder to shoulder in the narrow entry. "I'm Henry," he offered.

"Sadie." She couldn't think of anything else to say. They usually had a table between them, a distance she hadn't ever dared to cross.

Henry was drenched with sweat, like he'd been standing there a long time. "Well, this sucks. I guess I'll go home," Henry said. "Do you live close by? Do you want to come back to my house to cool off for a minute?"

Her heart started to race.

"It's just a few blocks away," he said. A bead of sweat fell from his dark hair onto the sidewalk, where it evaporated immediately.

"Sure," Sadie said, though it felt like someone else was saying it. What was she doing? But Henry couldn't tell how nervous she was, or he was being nice about it. He walked away and gestured to her. Sadie followed him out of the shade and into the blinding sun.

*

"This is my house," Henry said as they passed over the threshold. The house had shingles in different colors and a tower with big stained glass windows. It was on Sadie's way to the library, and sometimes there was strange music coming from the garage, so loud she could hear it over The Tape.

"We can get a drink inside and wait for my mom. She can give you a ride home," Henry said. He fidgeted with the earbuds hanging from one ear. "I should warn you. She's probably going to be weird. She teaches at the high school."

Sadie peered around the living room. It reminded her of the Weasley house. Every wall was covered in photographs and pictures: some of Henry, others of painted figures Sadie vaguely recognized. She found kings, generals, and heroes among the minor triumphs of kindergarten graduation and soccer team victories. Half an encyclopedia seemed to be papering the walls.

"What does she teach?"

"History," he muttered. Sadie's heart thumped. "Honors history. She has kind of a reputation, so people know her."

"Mrs. Vaughn?"

"Are you in high school?"

"I'm going to be in ninth grade. I just met her a few days ago for cross-country," Sadie said. Henry tossed his bag on the couch and sat on the bench in front of the piano.

"Oh, good luck with that. She's got kind of a reputation there too."

Sadie glanced around. It was weird, seeing a teacher's house. Kind of like looking at a teacher's diary.

"I'm going to be in tenth," Henry said. "Everyone says my mom is the best and the hardest, but I'm not in her class. Anyway. She might be weird."

He absentmindedly played an arpeggio, then sprang up as though he'd forgotten something and reached for her bag. Sadie stepped away, hugging her backpack full of secrets to her chest.

"My mom can give you a ride home," he said. "She'll be here in a few minutes. Or do you want to call your parents to pick you up?"

"I really don't need a ride," Sadie said. "I can walk." She backed into the door, startling herself.

"Oh, well, I thought . . . you know . . . we could hang out for a while. Since the library is closed."

Her heart was pounding in the unfamiliar room. Details piled themselves up around her begging to be analyzed, so many they seemed like static on a television.

"We could watch TV," Henry offered. At the sound of his voice her mind cleared. "I have a lot of cool anime DVDs. My dad is stationed in Okinawa. In Japan. I've been there."

"Okay," Sadie mumbled, but they didn't move. *What are you thinking!* screamed part of her brain.

"Or we could go sit on the porch and read and have some snacks," Henry said, trying again. Sadie didn't say a word. She had lost herself in the massive undertaking of reading the unfamiliar room: an armchair threadbare on one side, a Christmas ornament from Tokyo still hanging in hundred-degree weather, a pile of dusty sheet music. These things were invisible to him—the details so familiar they had faded into the background—but as a visitor, she could see them.

"You play guitar?" she asked, realizing how long she'd been staring. She pointed to the guitar leaning in its stand next to the piano.

"Oh, yeah. Classical guitar. And I'm kind of trying to start a band. I play the piano too."

Suddenly excited, he whirled around to face the keys. He plunked out the first few bars of "Blackbird," and opened his mouth to sing, his fingers deep in the keys.

"Not that!" Sadie cried.

"What? Oh, I thought you liked the Beatles."

"I do. I just . . . ," Sadie trailed off. "Wait, how did you know that?"

"Your tape player. Very vintage. I can hear it sometimes

through your earbuds when you take them off. I thought you liked the Beatles."

"I do. But I . . ."

But there was no way to explain to him why The Tape was special.

After a minute, Henry said, "Here, I'll get us some water." He vanished through a swinging door.

Free to observe, she lost herself in the walls and their mysterious pictures. She began to see George peeking out from the trenches, standing in the crowds.

Henry came back with a pink tray holding two giant glasses of water and a bowl of little mandarin oranges. He'd put a lemon wedge in each of the glasses, like they were in a restaurant.

"I wanted to make sure you had something to drink, because you can die of dehydration. That's what my dad says."

"I have water in my bag," Sadie replied.

He opened his mouth to say something, but then they heard the sound of keys in the door.

"Hello!" Henry's mom shouted, one arm wrapped around a yoga mat, the other wiggling the keys in the lock. She stopped, noticing the visitor.

"Mom, this is Sadie Black," Henry said. He ran to the door and took her gym bag.

"Oh, I know all about Miss Sadie Black. She's going to be quite the warrior this summer. Did you know, I went to WashU when your parents were there. They used to have a radio show. I wonder if they remember me." His mom finally freed her keys from the lock and hung them by the door.

"Nice to see you, Mrs. Vaughn," Sadie mumbled. She didn't remember telling Henry her last name.

"And nice to see you, Miss Black. Please, call me Liz. You're headed into ninth grade next year, right?"

"Yeah, she's a year behind me."

"I keep my eye on all the bright young eighth graders. I think I've even seen your name on my roster for class," she said with a wink.

"The air-conditioning broke at the library so they didn't open today, and I invited Sadie in for some water before she walks home. Or maybe we could give her a ride?"

"Sounds like a plan. It's too hot to be walking today. You like to hang out at the library, Sadie?"

"Yes," said Sadie hesitantly. Was that cool? Would Henry think she was sucking up to his mom?

"That's how we know each other," Henry added, beaming. "We're always at the library, so we see each other a lot."

"That's awesome," Mrs. Vaughn said. "Hey, how about we all go get some ice cream?"

"All right!" Henry shouted. Sadie didn't say anything. Was she supposed to refuse? She wasn't sure what would be the most polite. Anxiety climbed her spine, paralyzing her whole body.

"Sadie, do you want to call your parents and ask if it's all right?"

"No. They don't mind."

"Are you sure? Why don't you call. They might worry."

Sadie saw that she had a text from her mom asking how her day was going. She slid it aside and dialed the house phone so she would be sure to reach the voice mail. She explained the situation to the dead silence and waited until it sounded like someone had answered, then said, "Okay," and hung up. She could have called the shop. But what if they'd said no? She wasn't supposed to deviate from the plan. She didn't know why she did it. She knew her parents wouldn't have been mad; they were always encouraging her to make friends. But keeping secrets came naturally to her, like an instinct.

"Great!" said Mrs. Vaughn. "Let us sally forth. It is not the ice cream we shall conquer, but ourselves!"

"Mom!" Henry groaned.

"Edmund Hillary," Sadie said quietly. "He climbed Everest," she explained to Henry. She and George had climbed Everest once. She felt a flutter of icy snow on her neck, a tingle of an adventure. She could see the flakes falling around them.

"A double cone for the lady," Mrs. Vaughn said as they made their way outside. "You should know, my progeny: great men are made of great words."

"Dad says great men are made of great deeds," Henry countered.

"Those as well. But after their deeds, what is left but the stories we tell?"

Henry rolled his eyes and Sadie's snow melted away.

Henry's mom sat in the car while they stood in line. She pulled a book out of her Whole Foods tote bag. It was as big as the old dictionaries at the library. She put on her glasses and put her feet on the dashboard.

"This is great," Henry said. "We never go out for ice cream."

They walked up to the outdoor window of the white-washed building in silence. Henry didn't seem to notice how her stomach was full of butterflies—"Butterflies? Trite," George whispered in her ear— or how the under-arms of her Ravenclaw shirt were dark spots of sweat. He was bouncing on his toes, humming to himself. He almost looked nervous.

"What are you having?" asked the girl at the window when it was their turn.

"Small vanilla milk shake," Sadie mumbled.

"You can get a big one if you want," Henry said. "I have twenty dollars."

"I'm okay."

"No, really, it's my treat."

"*Come on,* guys," the girl said, and they realized they were holding up the line. "What are you having?"

They ordered their ice cream and perched on the chain-link fence like birds. It was so hot, half the city was in this parking lot. Henry seemed focused on his ice cream, so Sadie let George consume her. He sat next to her, sullenly letting his cone drip onto the sidewalk. Sadie felt better with him sitting there, though.

"Are you okay?" Henry asked. George vanished.

"What?"

"You seemed kind of zoned out."

"No, just thinking," Sadie said.

"You can get heatstroke pretty easily. That's what my dad says. He made me take all these survival and first-aid classes, so I know how to take care of you if you don't feel well."

He stared at his shoes. It was funny the way he started talking in facts, almost like Sadie did when she was nervous. It made him seem less scary, like a lost little kid.

"I'm okay. Thanks for the ice cream."

"Have you been here before?"

"Of course," Sadie replied.

"It's just ... you didn't go to school with everyone until ..."

"Yeah," Sadie said. He knew about the accident, she realized. Of course he knew who she was.

"I'm sorry. For asking, I mean. If you don't want to think about it—"

"My dad used to have this thing where he would tell me it was against the law for this place to serve kids under sixteen any size larger than a small," she told him, smiling so he wouldn't have to feel bad. "He bought me a large once after I was whining one day. Then he printed up a fake police ticket and mailed it to me, and I was like six so I thought it was real and I cried. He was really sorry."

"That's funny."

"He also told me he needed to sign a release for me to drink coffee and submit it to the American Bureau of Bad Parenting. And then I found out the coffee I was drinking was decaf all along anyway."

"Your dad sounds fun."

Sadie nodded. He didn't seem so uncomfortable anymore. She hated the look of pity she'd seen glinting in his eyes. It was an adult look.

"What's your dad like?" she asked.

"He's normal. My mom's the weird one."

"She seems nice."

"Yeah? Let's see how you feel at finals."

Their conversation stalled. It was weird sitting there alone together. She never felt weird alone with George. She wondered what the right thing to say to Henry might be. But she didn't know, so she didn't say anything.

"Thanks for coming with me," Henry said. He cleared his throat. "Can we hang out again tomorrow?"

"At the library?"

"Sure. Like always."

"Sure. Unless you have other plans."

"No, that is my plan," Henry said. "I mean, you're my plan."

He seemed to realize what his mouth had said a moment

too late to stop himself. He turned away and ran his fingers through his hair so it hid his face. Sadie turned away. She could hear her heart beating, or maybe it was his.

"So . . . cool?" he squeaked out. "Tomorrow?"

"Yeah," Sadie said. "I'll be there."

They exchanged numbers, but they didn't say anything else. All Sadie could think was *I'll see Henry tomorrow.* Every step was toward Henry tomorrow. Every moment ticked toward a future and Henry. The promise of tomorrow glowed so bright, it outshone the joy of being with him today. They piled back into the car, sweaty and sticky, and Mrs. Vaughn put down her book and drove them to Sadie's house. She knew where it was without Sadie having to tell her. Sadie wondered: what else did Mrs. Vaughn know?

Sadie struggled to unbuckle her seat belt as fast as she could, but Mrs. Vaughn turned around before she could escape.

"Are you signed up for any clubs yet?"

"Clubs?"

"Like, at school."

"*Mom.* Jeez!"

"No, I don't have a club," Sadie said, finally freeing herself. She made a break for the door, managing to get out, but—

"Great! I'll send your parents the forms for debate. You look like a talker to me."

"I'm not."

"I bet you are. The quiet ones always are. You just need a stage to shine on."

"Mom. *No.* Drive."

"Henry, stop being a pill. Sound good, Sadie?"

"Uh, sure," Sadie said, creeping away.

"I'm looking forward to seeing you this summer and in my class next year, Sadie. And you know, if you ever need someone to talk to . . ."

"Thanks," Sadie said. Henry was bright red as he shut the door. "Thanks for everything. I'll see you tomorrow, Henry."

✳

Her parents were still at the shop when Sadie got through the front door. She locked herself in, like Mrs. Vaughn might chase her up the driveway. She quickly erased the message she'd left on the machine, grabbed a soda from the fridge, and ran out into the backyard, nearly tripping on her parents' tools spread out on the unmowed grass around the truck. After the crash, her parents had taken a special interest in restoring Old Charlotte. They were determined to make her as good as new, and they'd gotten pretty far. On the outside, everything looked fine.

She climbed into Old Charlotte's backseat, her heart pounding and her mind fleeing in a million directions. She cleared off the books she'd abandoned in the back and lay down with her feet on the window.

She played through the day over and over, and every time she did, it seemed a little brighter. She stood where she'd stood in his living room, stuttered out cleverer lines, tasted ice cream that was better than ice cream ever could be. After a few minutes, her mind calmed down, and she took out her Walkman and put The Tape into Old Charlotte's tape player, coaxing the ignition into cooperation.

She stared at the stained felt ceiling. *Had* it been so wonderful? Or was he just being nice? It seemed so unlikely, that he'd be that nice. Why would he be that nice to her? The joyous circus of her mind started performing darker tricks—

"You know, I can play the piano too," George said from the driver's seat. He whisked them away to a deserted Moroccan bar. George cleared his throat and sat at the piano.

"I know," Sadie said, watching him desperately fumble to find the notes to "As Time Goes By." He gave up and slammed the lid.

"You like him," he said, his hair hanging over his face.

"Does he like me?"

"Of course. Don't be stupid. Can't you see how nervous he is?" he snapped.

"I don't think so."

"We *never* go out for ice cream," George mimicked cruelly.

"George!" Sadie snapped.

"Sorry," he said, shocked at his own outburst. He continued quietly: "Do you like him more than me?"

"No. Different than you."

George said nothing. He snapped his fingers and they

were back in the truck. Sadie leaned in to the front seat. She put a hand on his shoulder.

"Will we still go on adventures?" George asked.

"Of course. Always."

George held out his hand. Sadie shook it.

"Always," George said, turning up the volume on the stereo.

The speakers let out a screech and they both jumped. The Tape had ground to a halt. It slid halfway out of the stereo and then stopped.

"What's wrong with it?" Sadie asked.

"It's stuck."

"Oh no! George, can you fix it?"

George pushed buttons, tugged the cassette, applied all manner of witchcraft and wizardry, but Old Charlotte's only response was to swallow the rest of the tape. It wouldn't even play.

"At least it's not completely gone," Sadie said, holding the empty broken case in her hand.

"And we'll never have to worry that we'll lose it ever again. We'll always know where it is," George said brightly.

"But it . . . hurts," Sadie said.

"So it does."

"How can you just sit there smiling? Don't you care at all?"

"Of course I do. The trick, Sadie, is not minding that it hurts. Things will be lost. People will leave you. You have to keep going. That's life."

Her heart felt strangled. "Will I ever lose you?" she asked timidly.

"No, darling. No. Of course not. Everything but me."

But she was still crushed.

"Hey, I know. I'll sing it to you." George started singing softly. He knew The Tape just as well as she did. He passed his hand over the stereo, and it began playing along with him, every perfect note. Sadie lay down again in the backseat and listened, but it hurt to think about The Tape never coming back.

Sadie wanted so much not to hurt anymore that she made herself forget about The Tape. She closed her eyes tight and erased it from every summer, capsizing its memory and sinking it to the bottom of the black forgotten ocean. George stumbled over the lyrics and began humming, the music fading away. She closed her eyes and thought only of the good things that had happened that day. If she could only make herself forget the sadness, all that would be left was joy.

DAY 4

Ernest Shackleton was an Antarctic explorer. Someone once said, "For scientific leadership, give me Scott; for swift and efficient travel, Amundsen; but when you are in a hopeless situation, when there seems to be no way out, get down on your knees and pray for Shackleton." That's how awesome he was. He's not remembered for conquering Antarctica. He's remembered for surviving it against all odds.

When Shackleton's men were stuck on the ice without hope of land, without hope of rescue, and every single moment could be called a treacherous brush with death, they found to their surprise that things settled down pretty quickly. Only a few days after their ship, the *Endurance,* went down, they settled into routine and their sense of constant danger gave way to a sense of . . . boredom.

That's basically what's happened to me.

I am so bored. Everything in a hospital is very routine. Pain checks, check-ins, bed checks. You're expecting *One*

Flew Over the Cuckoo's Nest and it's just checkmarks on a whiteboard.

So I've been writing, and trying to edit what I'm writing here, because the TV doesn't have TCM and the only thing on is *Law & Order* in every flavor. We have a big library I could use, and it has a bunch of movies, but the nurses will not get me any DVDs, because I am theoretically capable of wheeling myself there and getting them myself.

My leg still hurts, but that's not why I won't go out there. It's that I don't want to see who's here. I'm hiding. I'm going home in two days, and if I just play my cards right, I can get out clean, unscathed, virtually scarless.

In here I'm safe.

But the only thing to do is write.

Maybe that's Roberts's evil plan. Bore me into writing down my secrets.

I look at this morning's entry, before I got off on that Shackleton tangent . . . How did that even happen?

I ate breakfast.

I cringe because it's true and if Roberts wants me to write true things, that's what she's getting, but it's just so dumb to write it down. Now I remember how I got distracted. I cross out "breakfast" and write in:

really weird-looking eggs that are the consistency of blubber

. . . because I thought that earlier and wondered what it would be like to eat blubber like they did on Antarctic missions. And then I got lost in all that stuff about Shackleton.

If I hadn't remembered to write it down, it would have been lost forever, that weird thought about blubber. And in a way, it's more true than just saying breakfast, even though it's probably wrong because I don't know what blubber really feels like. But saying it that way feels more real.

When I look up, Eleanor is standing right next to my bed.

I didn't even hear her come in.

We just kind of stare at each other for a second. You have to understand, she's not like normal people. You can't just say boring stuff like "Hey, how's it going?" to her. I mean, she's wearing her fleece shark costume with teeth hanging down over her head. It's beyond filthy, and all the teeth are stained and brown. It's the kind of thing that would seem like an affectation if anyone did it in school, like one of those cool kids who think they're so offbeat that society can't stifle their creativity, and they all listen to the same hipster music and read Sartre and practice Buddhism and threaten to kill themselves and stuff, and everyone knows they're the real A-list kids even though they say they're outcasts. Everything they do seems like watching a TV show, like they're asking you, "Am I interesting?" every time they get dressed.

But you look into Eleanor's eyes and see: this girl's the real deal.

So we just kind of sit there in silence for a long time, which is hard if you've ever done that. Silence is pretty much always uncomfortable for me, except with George, of course.

"We're going to be best friends," Eleanor says finally, as though we've been having a long conversation and this is its conclusion.

"Okay," I mumble. My heart is racing.

And then she erupts, chattering on about her various brushes with the law. Her mom is an artist and her dad is really rich, so she goes to boarding school in France. She hates boarding school because it's all so pretentious, but she misses her boyfriend. She's a criminal and an artist and schizophrenic and amazing. She hears voices and has spirits who follow her. They're totally real to her, she tells me. But she hasn't seen them since she got here because she's doped out of her mind.

"So what are *you* in for?" she asks.

"I crashed my car. Broken leg."

"No, what are you *in* for. What's your story?" She pokes me hard. Her arms are covered with thin white lines. They look so delicate I don't know what they are at first.

"I don't understand."

"Yeah you do. You know. I can see right through you."

I bite my lip.

"I broke my leg. It's just . . . standard procedure," I say, parroting back what I've been told. She gets off the bed and goes to the door.

"You know, we might be allies. But I need allies I can trust, Miss"—she consults the chart on my door—"Miss Sadie Black. And in the grand scheme of things, embracing the truth of your plight is likely to do more good than harm. You can't fight an enemy you don't understand."

She steps out of the room.

"Wait!" I call after her. She grins and returns to me.

"It's the silence that makes you crazy, you know? Who am I going to tell, anyway? No one would believe me. I'm psychotic. I'm a liar."

"Right. But I'm telling the truth." I think I am, at least. Sometimes I don't even know.

"Oh come on. You *want* to tell someone. Tell me. What is it? Raped by a football player? Alcoholic? Bulimic? Suicidal cry for help—"

"It's nothing! There's just been a misunderstanding about the car crash."

"Because of your friend."

"What?" My heart stops.

"The one you don't want to talk about."

"How do you know about that?"

She smiles. "I have my ways. I am invisible to those in power."

She raises her eyebrows expectantly.

I hold my breath. I grit my teeth, weighing the options. I know better. But then, there is something about being in the glow of someone interesting and watching her listen. Having her full attention is such a rush. My little life seems so magnified in her eyes.

I've never told this to anyone. Not even Lucie. Definitely not Henry. But my mouth is already moving, even though part of me is trying to choke back the words. Before I can stop myself, I reply faintly:

"His name is George. And he's . . . not real."

She cackles maniacally. "His name is George? Just George?"

"Well . . . yeah." George doesn't have a last name, I realize. I never considered it important.

"Is he a person or a monster or what?"

"A person. But he's just kind of an imaginary friend. Not like a hallucination or anything."

"Sure, sure. And what do you and George do?"

"We hang out," I say lamely.

"Do tell."

"Mostly we go places that I read about."

"How?"

"We just do. Haven't you ever daydreamed or . . . like . . . imagined something?"

"Sure," Eleanor says, exasperated. "But I want details! Details! Technical tips and tricks!"

I sigh. It's hard to explain.

"Well, I just . . . think about it," I say. "And then the thinking becomes daydreaming and the whole world fades away and I'm with George."

Right then, we hear footsteps. Our heads snap to the door like two meerkats.

"Cover for me," Eleanor whispers. I nod. She slips into the bathroom, where I can barely see her hair and shark fin in the mirror.

It's a nurse.

"Hello," I say.

"Was someone in here with you?"

"No."

She raises an eyebrow at me. "Are you sure? Dr. Roberts is going to be here in five minutes."

"Yes, I'm sure," I say, too formally for it to sound true. "I was, however, reading aloud."

"All right. By the way, a boy called—"

"I know," I say, clutching my T-shirt on instinct, like wringing his neck. "I'll call him later."

"He must be nice, such a sweet young Romeo, calling you all the time."

"That story doesn't end well," I tell her.

"Yes, but it begins so beautifully."

She sighs dramatically and leaves. I grin. She's not so bad.

"That was close," Eleanor says, apparating herself to my bedside. "The doctors here are morons, but the nurses have laser vision."

"Will you get in trouble for being in here?"

"More for poisoning the minds of America's youth. Don't worry, though. Roberts is a lamb compared to some."

"She's trickier than you think," I tell her. My notebook is under the covers and I run my fingers over its bony spiral binding. "She wants me to write down stuff about George. She thinks it'll make it easier for us to talk about . . . things. But I know she's going to use it against me."

"Why are you doing it, then?"

I think about it, and I don't have a good reason except . . . a person in a white coat told me to. Milgram experiment in action, I guess. Stanley Milgram did this famous experiment where a person dressed up like an authority figure told random people to give electric shocks to a stranger, and a lot of people did it even though they could hear the person screaming. Sometimes they kept going until the person stopped screaming altogether. I feel a little ashamed.

"Well . . . I refuse to write anything about George. It's too dangerous. But I can't really do what she wants, so it doesn't matter anyway," I tell her.

"Can't do what?"

"Write a story. A *true* story or whatever she said. I tried, but it sounds stupid."

Eleanor gets up and stands on the bed, towering over me. The movement from her standing shoots waves of pain up my leg, but I'm so stunned I barely notice.

"I'll bet it's a *great* story!" she shouts down at me. "But don't write it for them. Write it for me. I have an appreciation for the fine art of hallucination."

"He's really not a hallucination."

"Daydream, then, my little dreamer." She drops down. "So tell me about him."

"What do you want to know?"

"What does he look like?"

"I don't know. Like . . . a guy," I tell her. "He's got black hair and blue eyes."

"Is he hot?"

At this point, I notice Eleanor's pretty brown eyes, and the bloodshot whites. They reminded me of Henry's eyes when he gets offstage after a concert: the way he's completely disoriented and can't even hear me. He always looks like he's struggling to break through from some other world. I wonder where Eleanor is coming from.

I can see her toenails through her threadbare socks: bright red. I notice the pink bandages on her arm, and how they are covered in words I can't read, like they've been tightened and the words have been misaligned. And then I realize that she is staring at me, and I am staring at her and saying nothing, and so I have to answer her.

"I like his eyes," I say, still contemplating Eleanor more than George. Of course he is hot, in a way. But not in a way that is easy to explain. He's hot to me. It's like when you see a picture of someone you know well and they appear to be so much less than who they are to you. Describing him ruins it all.

"Tell me about them! Specifics!"

It's strange. It's hard to pull his face to my mind even though I knew it so well. I am filled with Eleanor.

"Well, they're blue."

"Blue how?"

"Blue . . . like the ocean."

"Like the ocean? That's called a *cliché*. You can't describe someone's eyes like they're the ocean, unless you go full *Princess Bride* and they're like the sea after a storm."

"Well, what if it's true?"

She taps her temple, thinking.

"I suppose if the truth is a cliché, then . . . you must accept it no matter how boring. Or trite," she concludes.

I don't like that. Nothing about George is a cliché.

"Well, it is true," I start, thinking of his eyes. Blue could be so many things, if you really paid attention. "But they're a totally original kind of blue, just like the ocean is new every day. Sometimes they're ice-blue like the polar seas. Sometimes they're blue as water over white sand. Sometimes they're blue like the deep ocean where the fish that light up live. Dark blue. Dangerous blue. They're blue like they could capture a ship for Davy Jones's locker, and all the pirates would never care that they were dead because they would have gotten to see that perfect shade of nocturnal ocean blue."

She grins.

"Blue like *that* ocean is certainly not a cliché."

"I've never seen the ocean." It's true: in all our family trips, we never made it to the coast.

"Could have fooled me."

"Me too," says a voice from the door.

Dr. Roberts is standing there, looking in on us.

"I'm afraid I'll have to steal Sadie for a while," says Dr. Roberts.

Eleanor leans in close.

"Promise me you won't tell her a thing. Save your stories for me," Eleanor hisses. She spits a little in my ear, but I don't mind.

I nod.

"Eleanor, you're not supposed to be in here," Roberts says, her hand sweeping toward the door. "You girls are welcome to socialize in the common room."

"I knew you were special," Eleanor whispers in my ear. And off she swims, a shark on land.

✳

"Did you write your story?" Roberts asks, settling herself in.

"It's not done," I tell her.

"Oh? But that means you are working on it, right?"

I don't want to tell her about my brilliant "true" observations:

Nothing is on TV.

My socks are blue.

I want pizza.

105

I just give her my most masterful sullen-teenager stare. She clears her throat. I win.

"So what would you like to talk about today?"

"Nothing."

"How about some coloring. It's very trendy right now. You're going home in a few days. Could be a new hobby?"

She pulls some blank paper and an impossible quantity of crayons and pencils out of her briefcase of secrets. It must be bottomless to fit all that. She sets some on the little table I have across my bed.

"Are we going to do that stupid thing where you ask me to draw a house and a tree and it reveals my darkest secrets?"

She laughs.

"We can draw a house if you want to. Here: draw me your house, and I'll draw something for you too. Then you can know all my darkest secrets as well."

"Fine."

"Shall we listen to some music? I have these speakers. . . . I noticed you have an iPod."

"It's a mix from my boyfriend. He sent it to me."

"Oh? I heard there's someone who keeps calling you, but you won't take the call. Is that Henry?"

"Yes," I groan. "It's Henry. My boyfriend, Henry."

"Not George?" I can practically hear her salivating.

"No. It's Henry calling. And the music's not private. It's just his music and some bands we like. You can listen to it if you want to," I say. She pulls out the speakers and I plug the iPod in to shut her up. In an instant the air is full of pure electrified punk rock. She cringes. One point to me. Some of Henry's favorite music is hard to like.

We settle in and start drawing, but I can see her watching me, so I don't know how many of her deepest darkest secrets are going on that paper. I try to focus, but my thoughts start to wander as I draw. I can't get lost now, especially with her sitting right across from me. I have to be careful. There's no way I can get away with daydreaming right in front of her. I focus as hard as I can on my house.

I start with the basement, where I draw two big squares: one for my room, and one for the laundry/storage place where all our old stuff is in boxes. It's kind of like the part of a museum that's off display, like our archives or something. After the crash, all of my parents' travel and radio stuff got put in the basement: the records and suitcases and cassette tapes.

In my room, I draw little rectangles for the bookcases and my bed, and a little circle for my beanbag chair, where I like to sit and read. I draw the stairs up as even, neat lines. On the ground floor the kitchen becomes a geometry problem of cooking ephemera my mom never uses. The little island that used to host all my dad's and my projects—Lego fortresses and Hot Wheels death circuits—rises in the middle of it. The living room, the bathroom, the master bedroom, all in a ring. The great big TV is reduced to a thin little rectangle from above. On the second floor, I outline my dad's cave and my mom's craft room—which are remarkably similar in their contents—and the other bathroom. I'm kind of fuzzier on those rooms. My parents shut themselves in their offices just like I shut myself in the basement. I write their names on their boxes instead.

Outside is where Old Charlotte used to be, so I fence in our yard and draw her in even though she's gone.

That's it, I think. *That's everything.*

It looks awfully empty like that.

So I go back to the boxes in the basement and label them. Sometimes I forget that we have a second floor of the house. Our boxes I never forget.

Our whole life from before is in those boxes, but my parents don't care. It's nothing but a bunch of old junk to them now. Now they listen to classical music and NPR and run a respectable business. That's what was fated for us, I guess. Besides all the records and all the things you need to play them, we have the whole collection of Mom's Beatles stuff that you can't imagine was easy to find in the 1970s when she was a kid. Like, Beatles shoes and cups and pins and pictures. She has newspaper clippings from when John Lennon was shot. Real ones, not even printouts. She has all these posters she made out of cut-up pictures, and all these drawn-over books of guitar tabs with her handwritten notes on them.

My dad's got all his days on the road in boxes down there too: camp stoves, suitcases, cool old sleeping bags and stuff.

He always wanted to take road trips when he was a teen-ager. My parents were going to live in a VW van at one point and just see the whole world. They thought they were going to have the most mobile life you could build, without furniture, without rules, without anything. Their lives were going to be motors and music and me. We were going to be vagabonds forever. It all packed up very nicely in the end.

I look at my drawing and it feels small because it is small. So I draw in every single thing I know is in our house, even the things I don't really notice anymore: fancy pillows on the bed, the lamp in the living room, the windows and doors and chairs. My mom buys tons of furniture now, so I have lots of things to draw. I lose myself completely in the details and when I remember I'm supposed to be focused and not give anything away, Roberts is looking at my paper.

"Sorry, I didn't mean to interrupt," she says.

"It's fine." I shove the paper at her. "There's the house. Are we done?"

"You're very precise," she says, examining it. She hands me hers. It's two sticks with a roof, basically, and some flowers in the yard. It looks kind of like a little kid drew it. "Most of the time people draw the outside of the house. It's interesting that you drew the floor plan," she says.

"Yep. Fascinating. I'm probably a serial killer," I say. Roberts laughs.

"Well, what do you think it means?"

"Probably about as much as the fact that you drew red flowers in front of yours."

"I have red flowers in my yard right now. They're my favorite part of my house. I love all these details in yours. You must really care about your house. What are these empty boxes up here, though?"

"My parents' offices. I didn't finish them."

"Why?"

"Why are you making me do these stupid things? Write a story? Draw a picture?"

"I asked you to do it. I'm not making you do it."

"But why?"

"Because we sometimes . . . reveal ourselves in what we write or draw or say or do, in ways we can't see, ourselves, very easily. And when we talk with another person, we may figure out things we wouldn't have realized any other way."

"But I don't want to 'reveal myself.' I want you to just believe me when I tell you I wasn't trying to kill myself. Because that's the truth. That's my true story: I crashed my car into a tree and it was an accident. The end."

"So, why *don't* you want to do it, then?" I rush to answer and she holds up her hand. "And don't say because it's stupid . . . think about it for a second."

I do. I wait a long time so she'll think I've delved really deep into my subconscious, and then I tell her:

"My English teacher made one of the exam questions last year 'Why did Mary Shelley write *Frankenstein*?' The answer was, Mary Shelley wrote *Frankenstein* because she was afraid of childbirth. Like it was a fact. Not like she sat down to tell a story, but like she just sat down and said,

'I'm afraid of childbirth, and hence I shall write *Franken-stein.*'

"I don't think people write stories like that. And it's kind of rotten, to just disregard that she wrote a really kick-ass scary story. It's like the story doesn't even matter. And I don't know if you ever even get to know what you *mean* when you tell a story. But you can know what you're *saying*. And I just think that we should look at the facts, and take people at their word."

"But that's exactly the point, isn't it? That maybe we can see something new as readers."

"But how could we ever know that it's true?"

"We can't," she says, shrugging. "Just like I can never really know what's inside your head. All I can do is provide . . . feedback. Help you identify themes, ask questions, challenge suppositions . . . but you're writing this story. You can write a lot of stories from the same facts. It's interesting to look at which one you choose to tell."

Dead end. Obvious trap. Abort mission.

"So what do you think of my house?" I ask.

She looks at it for a moment, then she tucks it into her briefcase to be analyzed with the rest of me.

"Honestly? What I'm wondering is . . . what you stand to gain by changing the subject."

Oh, Dr Roberts. You must love us teenage girls. So ready to break at any moment. So ready to erupt into a fountain of answers if only someone would listen. If only someone would speak that one sentence that is so insightful it cuts through the sarcasm. You must love the challenge. The puzzle. Just what is wrong with Sadie Black?

Well, fat chance she'll be finding out. I will outsmart her. It's nothing personal. That's simply how it is. She's the enemy—

"Sadie? You're wandering, aren't you?" she says, and I snap to attention.

"What?"

"You looked like you were somewhere else."

"No."

"Sadie. Don't you think people can see when your thoughts are somewhere else?"

"I'm not crazy!"

"No one said you were."

Blunder. If this were a game of chess, what I just did was a blunder. Roberts takes the board. Black flips the board onto the floor. Chess pieces everywhere.

"I don't think you're crazy," she says after an awkward minute.

"Then what do you think?"

"I think you're complicated, and you're trying to figure some stuff out."

And then, for some reason, I smile.

✳

"I think you're complicated," she told me so sweetly, like a serpent, "and you're trying to figure some stuff out."

Then I smiled because I'm an idiot. She almost got me.

I outsmarted Roberts for now, but I must be careful. Every moment is a battle. I have to remember that.

I stop before I write something I will regret. I'm trying to remember it all, to observe everything like an explorer, but it's almost impossible.

See, even explorers fail at that. It's like, if you climb Mount Everest, a lot of that time is alone in your head walking. But do people write down step after step? No, they write down the interesting parts. That's just how a journal works. It's exactly like the pain in my leg: every day is full of it, punctuated by little moments of talking, little checkmarks on a sheet. Sometimes exciting things happen. But mostly the adventure is pain.

Pain is the measure of my time, like steps taken on a journey. But I won't remember that. Or rather, I'll remember, but I won't *feel* it. Even when I write it down, it doesn't make it real to the person I will be in the future.

I am in constant pain.

See, that doesn't carry that pain forward. It's just a statement. The word *pain* is just the shadow of a stranger who's already gone.

I could paint a better picture, and maybe I could feel it then. Maybe I could carry that pain out of myself and into another person. But do I want to remember that? Or do I want to let it go?

What is it possible to save with words?

George. George. George. I write his name down as faintly as possible, but even that doesn't bring him here. *George* written down is just a word. Like pain.

I stop and stare at the page.

I completely mark out those featherlight words in black just in case. I know better than to write even his name.

My heart is pounding. What was I thinking? If I write his name and Roberts sees it, they'll take George away. If I tell Roberts about George, he will die.

I black out half the page around where I wrote his name, destroying everything near it. Just to be safe.

It would be nice, though: storing George in my notebook just in case. But if I came back, if I read what I wrote, would I even be the same me who wrote these words? Could I resurrect him from a few scribbled lines? I don't know if I could even save George by putting him in this journal.

But what else can I do?

George has always lived in my head. I never thought that was an unsafe place for him to be. I never thought—never even imagined—that anyone could take my thoughts from me. But Eleanor says they can steal your dreams, and I think she knows. This place I'm in, it can change what you think. It can uncover your deepest treasures and take them away. It can make things that once made sense to you unrecognizable. It can make you a different person, and those things you didn't write down . . . they're just gone.

What would I do if I lost the Star Palace forever? What would I do if I somehow lost George?

Dr. Roberts made me smile. She found a crack.

I can't talk about George, because then everyone will know I'm crazy. They will take my thoughts away, fix me. I live a beautiful life of shattered options, coexisting all at once, all of them unreal. I know that sounds crazy, but I'm not insane. You'd have to be insane not to want this.

George and I have lived in hundreds of worlds and hundreds of books. We passed our O.W.L. exams side by side. There are no mountains we have not scaled, no oceans we have not explored, and yet still there's infinitely more to see. He's taken me to Amsterdam countless times, to drink countless bottles of stars. I don't know why I live this way, but I can't stop. I'd die without George. I'd be empty.

My hand hovers over my notebook. Am I strong enough to walk out of here with George safe inside my head? Maybe a message in a bottle, to some future me, is his best shot.

Maybe if I wrote down our stories and did the best I could, made them as beautiful as they felt, I would be able to find him again.

I try to remember without going to him. I try to think of what it looks like from the outside, so I don't get sucked under. In these memories, I am a character in my own story, and that character is behaving . . . strangely.

Sadie hadn't gotten out of bed for days. She had been lying on the bottom of a black ocean.

I stop. I don't want to think about this. And anyway, I could never capture what it feels like to be with him. I'm not good at anything, not even telling my own story. Why bother to try?

Instead I write George a note that no one else could understand.

I am so sorry. I'm sorry I let myself get us here, and I'm sorry for every time you have called me and I have turned away. I am yours, and you are mine. I want us to have forever, to seek and find.

THE MARAUDER'S MAP

The ice extended beyond her line of sight, and had she not come from a world of hearths and tea, Sadie would not have believed in the existence of those comforts. The harshness of the landscape was complete, all-encompassing. It erased the rest of the world, leaving only the challenge: Antarctica. Never before had such a journey been attempted, not even by Shackleton, Amundsen, or Scott. She had to be strong. She was the only girl on this voyage, and a stowaway to boot. She couldn't just be a sailor. She had to be more.

Sadie squelched in her shoes as she marched with determination toward the captain sullenly sitting on his throne of snow. He gazed off into the white, battered by the icy wind. The only monument to civilization remaining—their ship trapped in the ice—stood behind him, and the rest of the crew gazed on as it creaked and finally began its descent into the black depths below, carrying its flag with it.

"Your coffee, Captain," she said, marching up with the insufficient cup of hot liquid. George drew himself up and tried to make himself look unperturbed. He took the coffee expertly, despite the layers and layers of coats and mittens. Only his blue eyes were visible through his thick hat and many scarves. He cleared enough of his face to speak.

"Are you afraid to die, girl?"

"No, Captain."

"And the others?"

"Not a man aboard is a coward. In fact, they are celebrating. They are singing."

George listened hard, and through the Arctic wind he pulled out the notes of a familiar song.

"Why do they sing?"

"After all the waiting, all the indecision, the end is in many ways a relief, sir. Even to die is better than the dullness of waiting."

"Ah, but it is not the end. We didn't go down with the ship after all."

He took a swig of coffee, glaring at her disdainfully.

"It's the start of an adventure," Sadie said. "It's what we're here for."

"Is that what you're here for?" he asked. He pulled his scarf down around his neck, breathing vapor thick as ghosts.

"Yes, Captain!" she nearly shouted. Her heart yearned for it: to see sights unseen, to face danger in every moment, to do what had never been done before.

"Are you sure it isn't . . . something else? Some*one* else?"

Sadie crinkled her nose, breaking character.

"What? George, what are you—"

He put an arm around her shoulder and she felt hot, too hot. This was wrong. This wasn't the adventure they were supposed to be on.

"Would you like to stay for dinner?"

"What?"

"Sadie, are you listening?" George started to melt, his charcoal hair dripping to the ground. Both George and the Antarctic waste evaporated and Sadie was back in reality. In the sweltering heat on his back porch, Henry asked: "Do you want to stay for dinner, or do you have to go home?"

Sadie put down her copy of Shackleton's *South*.

"I can stay," she said.

"You seem kind of out of it." He put down his book. He was supposed to be doing summer reading for school—the rising juniors were reading British everything—but hadn't made much progress. Sadie had finished hers for sophomore world lit months ago.

"Sadie?" he called her. "Where are you?"

"What?"

"In your head, I mean. You just seem like you're somewhere else." He frowned.

"I'm not."

Anger flickered across his face, though it evaporated in mere seconds. "Why do you always lie to me when I ask what you're thinking?" he asked.

"I don't."

George grinned icily in the back of her mind. *Yes you do,* he whispered.

Henry's eyes were boring into her, searching for the part of her that dreamed. All of her freshman year, Henry had been pacing her labyrinths trying to find her monsters, her secrets. She could never let her guard down. He must never find out.

"I was just reading," she said finally. "Really. You know I get distracted."

"Yeah, but you've been reading that page for a long time."

"So have you," she snapped. She covered her mouth, shocked at her own anger. Were they going to have a fight?

But she looked so shocked that Henry burst out laughing.

"Guilty as charged. You've seen through my clever ruse," he said with a grin. "The book was but a prop in my covert surveillance operation. You know, you make the funniest faces when you're reading."

Sadie turned bright red. How long had he been watching her? How long had she been with George? Her brain scrambled as she tried to think clearly: had her lips been moving? Had she been smiling strangely? What could he possibly have seen?

"I was just . . . you know . . ."

"Thinking?" he interjected.

"Yeah."

"I make faces when I listen to music, especially if I'm

trying it out in my head . . . awesome guitar solos and stuff. My mom calls it my 'crazy guitar look.' What were you thinking about?"

"Antarctica," Sadie said half-truthfully.

"Cool."

"Ice-cold, actually."

He laughed in the kind of ugly way she loved—all nose—throwing his head back like it was the funniest thing in the world. "Hey," he said, stopping. "Maybe instead of staying here for dinner we could go out. Like a real date."

Sadie paused, clutching her book to her chest.

"If you want to stay in, that's cool too," Henry said, eyeing the book. "But it's the last weekend before school. . . ."

"No, let's do it." She put the book down. So much had changed over her freshman year. She had been terrified of high school, but it had all worked out: she had two best friends. *Scratch that,* she thought. *A best friend and a* boyfriend.

"Awesome," Henry said, jumping up. He pulled Sadie up by the arm and her book fell under the porch swing. "There's this cool place I want to show you. Have you ever been to the Loop?"

"Yeah, there's a record store there that my parents like."

"Oh. Vintage Vinyl." His face fell.

"Yeah. But that's the only spot I know. We never hang around."

"Really?" he asked, brightening. "Excellent. I'm going to show you something you've never seen before."

Mrs. Vaughn and Sadie's parents had not been particularly approving of their plan, but after much pleading they reached a compromise on the matter of riding bikes home in the dark, and they were off. "I'll have my license soon," Henry assured her, but Sadie didn't mind. They pedaled hard up the hills, flying down them at breath-stealing speeds. It was farther than Sadie had ever ridden, extending the boundaries of what she considered possible. They took a scenic detour through Forest Park, riding past the art museum, and Sadie finally realized how close it was. It had never occurred to her that she could go there without her parents dropping her off and picking her up. But why not?

She missed museums. She'd been spending so much time with Henry, and it just wasn't his thing. But she missed her time alone in echoing halls of wonder. The world inside a museum was managed on a map. It was labeled and framed. There was something comforting about a frame and all that lies inside it. There was something comforting about a collection and the keeping of it. From fossils to paintings to skeletons, everything in a museum would live on forever, remembered. The past and present were only rooms apart, always accessible. Museums brought the world inside and organized it, kept it safe. That never changed.

"We could do this every day," said George beside her, leaning effortlessly over the handlebars of his vintage cruiser. There wasn't a drop of sweat on him. "Imagine how quiet it is inside. No one to bother us in there. We could explore the whole Antarctic."

Sadie smiled at the idea. They'd come back sometime, but not today.

"Come on!" Henry called, and Sadie rode past George.

They weren't far from where her family had been in the car crash. That day had become a hazy memory. The place was green and healed over. There weren't any scars left from the crash.

"What's up?" Henry asked, looking at her inquisitively. He handed her a bottle of water. "You look dazed."

"Nothing." Henry looked away. They'd already gone over this today. Sadie paused, though, taking a sip of water. Something was bubbling up inside her. "My family was in a car accident near here."

"I know. My mom remembers," Henry said. He looked around. Sadie was sorry she'd brought it up.

"I guess your parents were really hurt," Henry said hesitantly. "Don't they still have physical therapy? My mom said the other driver was, like, a teenager or something."

"Yeah," Sadie said.

"Do you ever think about what happened?"

Sadie didn't answer. She was receding into it, the final moments echoing in her head. It was better to say nothing than to tempt the memories. The distinction between past, present, and future was only an illusion, after all. That was what Einstein had said. That quote had colonized her like a cancer: she could never escape the past, nor exile it from the future. It was there, always, beneath the veneer of reality, a story waiting to be told, connections waiting to be made.

"Do you know where it was?" Henry asked. The present around her began to wash away into the past—

"I don't want to think about it," Sadie said softly, shaking her head and closing her eyes. "Let's just . . ."

"Yeah. Let's just," Henry said. He put his arm around her but she pulled away, still shaking off her thoughts.

"Sorry," she said, reaching out for his hand. He smiled, but with a question in his eyes that he knew he couldn't ask.

They pedaled on, escaping the difficult things.

They rode in silence and finally emerged on a bustling street. "Ta-da! The Delmar Loop," Henry said.

"What is it?"

"It's just a street. Good stores. Stuff that I like. Like Vintage Vinyl. They have an absolutely sick bargain bin that I need to hit up, but there's so much more."

It was already dusky, in the way that summer nights grew hazy long before dark. It made everything look like a noir film. They locked their bikes and strolled up the sidewalks to a large, bright window full of books. The display was full of detective novels, with a giant magnifying glass made of cardboard and all sorts of prop weapons.

"Okay, so, this is an awesome bookstore. Like, way better than the ones we've been going to in the mall. It's got so much crazy stuff, and old books, and weird books. My mom comes here a lot and I always think of you."

Sadie looked in the window: shelves and shelves of books, just like any bookstore, but it was different somehow. The light was warmer. The people inside had tattoos and wore vintage jackets. They were laughing, talking with the lady behind the desk, whose hair was buzzed short and who wore white lace gloves that in no way matched her outfit. Sadie could practically see that lady getting dressed in the morning in her black skinny jeans, putting each hand finger by finger into those crocheted gloves before she walked out the door to her motorcycle. She probably even crocheted them herself.

When Sadie looked around, she could see stories on all of the faces through the glass. She saw a few Truman State hoodies under a sign that read EXISTENTIALISM, and even spotted a girl from cross-country—a varsity girl from the front of the pack who played a few other sports—inside with her mom looking at giant art books. Sadie knew the pleasure of those books, how they were delightfully heavy in her lap at the library. She spiraled away into thoughts of what that girl was really like, if she too loved the weight of what she held. Sadie didn't know her. The girl caught her eye and waved, nearly dropping the enormous book in her arms. Sadie was knocked out of her thoughts. Had she been caught staring? She waved back but too late. The girl had escaped back into the pages. Henry sighed happily.

"Isn't it cool?"

"So cool," Sadie said. "This whole street. It's so different from where we live."

"Yeah, but you must have seen all kinds of interesting places traveling around with your parents for car shows."

"Not really," Sadie admitted. "Mostly just small towns in, like, rural Idaho and Ohio. Mostly gas stations and cornfields. But we always went to any museums or cultural things there were. My dad called them field trips."

"Like art museums?"

"Yeah, and science museums in Chicago and Detroit and stuff. And all the weird little town historical societies. Those are cool too, because you get to see the life of a whole town. It's like looking in other people's windows and thinking about their lives."

"Do you miss it?"

"Miss what?"

"Exciting places."

"It was just Ohio."

"That's where I want to go to school! Ohio is sick."

Sadie laughed a little nervously. Henry was going to be a junior. He was already planning for college, taking prep courses. "Oberlin is sick. Ohio is a lot of corn."

"You'll be able to drive then, you know. You can come visit me."

"Yeah," Sadie said. Thinking about it made her sad.

"What's wrong?"

"It's just . . ."

"Yeah?"

"I don't understand . . . why you even like me."

"What?"

"Like, you could meet someone awesome at Oberlin. You don't have to . . . to settle. . . ."

"I never settle," Henry said, laughing.

"But why me?"

He fidgeted with his hands, playing chords in the air. He wasn't good at saying things out loud. He said everything in notes and chords and harmonies.

"Maybe it's that . . . you've got things you love, like I love them. Like, if I have an album I'm obsessed with, you've got a book that goes with it. It's kind of like we fit together."

Sadie blushed. The people on the other side of the glass continued their shopping, oblivious to this time-stopping moment outside their window.

"Why do you even like *me*?" he asked her back.

Sadie laughed. She slid her hand into his, fingers twining.

"It's so obvious," she told him.

"But you can still . . . say it."

"Because you're . . . perfect. Who wouldn't like you?"

"But why do *you*?"

Sadie opened her mouth, but Henry held up a hand.

"That's your quoting face," he said with a grin. "You always say everything perfectly, but you never say it as you. I just mean . . . why do you like me? Like, in everyday words."

Sadie searched her mind. Everything she could come up

with was stolen from a movie or a book or a Beatles song. And that wasn't why. That was just a filter on why. But the filter was better than she could ever be, and she lost herself in a slide show of disguises for how she really felt: "You were my first friend. And then when you fell in love with me, I was so proud," she imagined saying. And then "Whatever our souls are made of, yours and mine are the same." On and on she went until she was lost in a rainstorm of words—

"It's okay," Henry said with a laugh, breaking her spiral of thoughts. "I know you do. Like me, I mean."

"Sorry," Sadie said. "I do like you. I like your . . . everything."

"Same."

"Double same."

He sighed, and instead of tripling or even taking her "same" to infinity in his usual silly way, he continued:

"It's just . . . I don't know why, but I always feel like you're far away. My mom once said you were homesick for the road."

"What does that even mean?"

"I don't know. I just thought . . . maybe you liked somewhere else better."

"I didn't really like anyplace in particular. Except . . ." She remembered, despite herself, how much she'd loved always moving, always being on an adventure. She remembered the promise of a different life broken against a tree in Forest Park. The sound of screaming tires—

"But this is cool, right? You like it?"

"Yeah," Sadie said quickly. He looked so desperate. Anyway, Ohio was nothing compared to Japan, where Henry's dad lived. What was she lamenting?

Sadie inspected the cracks in the sidewalk.

"So . . . do you want to go in?" Henry asked.

Sadie peered inside at the shelves and shelves of adventures. She could imagine George stocking the books, working undercover. She belonged in there, alone with the stories and George. She saw him, his back turned, putting books on shelves.

Then she turned to Henry.

"Maybe another time. This was perfect, though."

"Are you sure?"

"Let's eat. I'm figuratively starving."

＊

"Chuck Berry used to play at Blueberry Hill every once in a while," Henry said. "But mostly I like it for the cheeseburgers." Even so, it was "pretty freaking sweet," he thought, to eat in the places where his heroes had stood. He had told her the long history of Chuck Berry and rock and roll and its relationship to a variety of other genres between mouthfuls of Sadie's abandoned fries. They hadn't needed two appetizers after all, and the blueberry pie—"We have to! It's got blueberries!" insisted Henry—was definitely ill-advised, but they took it home. Laden with Styrofoam boxes and high on laughing and sugar, Sadie couldn't imagine how the night could have been more perfect.

Wandering away from the restaurant in the falling dark, Henry called his mom to come pick them up. Sadie glanced in store windows at their reflection. They looked almost like college students, almost like a real couple. Henry wrapped his arm around her shoulder.

"Twenty minutes," he told her. "We should get the bikes."

Sadie nodded, but she wasn't listening. She was looking at the building where they had stopped.

It was a movie theater, but not like the big theaters in the mall. She looked up and a neon sign sprang to life: TIVOLI. She'd heard her dad mention it once or twice, but they'd never gotten around to actually going.

The light from the box office lit up their faces. She backed up into the shadows to read the showtimes, leaving Henry standing under the neon lights.

"They're playing *Casablanca,*" she said.

"They're always playing *Casablanca* or some other old movie. It's that kind of theater."

"*That* kind of theater" rang in her ears. She bit her lip.

"Have you ever seen it? *Casablanca*?" he asked.

"It's a classic," Sadie said, trying to seem indifferent.

"I've never seen it. Did you like it?"

What if he thought she was weird? What if he stopped liking her? What if? What if?

"Yeah," she admitted. "Yeah. A lot."

"Oh, cool," he said, oblivious to her nervous shaking. "It looks like it's playing all week if you don't mind seeing it a second time."

She didn't correct him on the "second time." *Try twentieth,* she thought.

"It's in black-and-white," she warned him.

"Yeah, I know," he said, poking her.

He put his arm around her, and they looked at the movie posters on the side of the building. They were mostly for movies Sadie had seen in hotel rooms on TCM. In all of the posters, colorized black-and-white heroes sprang to adventure or gazed into the eyes of their romantic leads. Henry's arm was uncomfortably warm, but she liked it even in the summer heat.

Henry kissed her cheek. She jumped, staring at him. They never kissed in public. He was changing the unspoken rules. His grin fell, mistaking her surprise for horror.

Sadie glanced around, then kissed him back in kind. He kissed her awkwardly on the lips: a closed-mouth movie kiss. They smiled and stopped, looked around. No catastrophe had struck. It surprised them both, and they laughed, knowing they were thinking the exact same thing. They stood in front of the theater, a world of possibilities before them.

As they wandered away, the heroes' faces on the posters changed. In each, a pair of jilted blue eyes watched them. Though she didn't know why, Sadie felt a chill run through her entire body, right through her love-stricken heart.

DAY 5

I've begun to get curious about Eleanor.

Here is what I know about Eleanor. She is a shark. She is amazing. But who is she? How did she get here?

Maybe I'm curious a little too late. I want to know everything about her.

When she arrives in my room, I don't let her distract me with questions. I start right in with my own interrogation.

"Why are *you* here? I mean, I get that you have visions, but why are you here now?"

Her eyes darken. "Oh you know. It's not interesting," she says, flashing her wrists at me to say: it's obvious.

"When you hallucinate, what is it like?" I ask shyly.

"Beautiful." A nostalgic smile crosses her face. "And scary. And magic."

"Do you have hallucinations all the time?"

"No. But I get lonely without them."

"I'm lonely without George," I offer, more honestly than I intended. "I feel really alone."

"You are, and so am I. That's why we've got to stick together. They'll take everything you have, and you won't even realize it. And then you'll be alone forever."

Alone forever. The words threaten to wake up the unexploded bombs in the back of my mind. I quiet the memories and return to the present.

"How long have you known George?" she asks.

I blush. Before he was George, he was a million fragments of stories: the princes from books, the best friends, the heroes. He was there to save me when I was scared and alone. Every vanquisher of nightmares was George. But he wasn't George yet, he was only an idea.

But there was a point in which all those universes collided. Suddenly he had a name, and that is what made him real to me.

I love remembering when I met George. Sometimes I go back in my mind and watch it, like an iconic movie clip that makes you feel the whole movie run through you like a drug.

It was my first week back in regular school, back in seventh grade. I was staring into the pages of *Harry Potter and the Sorcerer's Stone.* I knew it so well I didn't even have to really read it to know where I was. I was just hiding in the pages, hiding at Hogwarts.

A teacher came to my desk.

"What are you doing?" she asked. I remember her being

terrifying, but I bet she was nice. I couldn't even answer, I was so scared.

"Can we put the book away during class, please?" she said. "You need to look at the board." She took my book away and put it on her desk. Then I remembered that I was supposed to be looking intently at a bunch of fractions.

The whole class laughed and I put my hands in my lap and counted, because I liked counting a lot then. I would count up and down until I lost all track of time, and whatever was bothering me was gone. But even counting wasn't enough to help this time.

Wouldn't it be nice to have someone who understands, I thought. I wanted it more than anything. But I knew that kind of thing didn't happen. Not in real life, anyway. In real life, every single person was alone.

But I could imagine what having someone like that would be like. I loved reading about partners in crime, about duos, about friends. Someone to watch your back and save you at the last second. That was what I wanted.

And then something magic happened: I watched a long shadow stretch and grow across my desk. I looked down under my desk at that shadow's glossy black shoes, and I saw myself reflected in them. I looked up and saw a face I felt I already knew. I didn't smile, but he did.

He doesn't feel so tall now, but back then he felt like a giant. He was wearing a black suit and a clean white shirt. I felt like I'd seen his eyes before.

"You know, Sadie, I think we're going to be the best of friends," he said.

"How did you know my name?"

"I know everything about you. You're the most fascinating person I've ever met."

"Sadie!" the teacher snapped, and I realized I had been staring, mumbling to myself, totally zoned out in a daydream.

I felt all the potential in the world leaking out at the seams, and the whole universe going gray. When my person vanished, he took all the color with him back to where stories and dreams lived.

So that day in class when I closed my eyes I made a million wishes to no one. I wished for a person all my own, who would never leave me, who would understand. And when I opened my eyes, I imagined that the boy was there. I knew he was imaginary, but it didn't matter.

"What is your name?" I asked, carefully keeping my face in the real world perfectly still. I didn't move a muscle.

His mouth made a half-crooked smile that stretched into his eyes, across his face, and infected me. And for the first time in a long time, I really smiled.

"My name is George," he said.

Nothing has been the same since.

"Cool," Eleanor says when I've told her all that. "So cool."

"I know," I admit, because come on, how awesome is

that image? I love living it, I love watching it, I even some-times improve on it. The kids get meaner, my clothes get cuter, George gets more and more heroic.

In my heart of hearts, though, I know that's not the first time George and I met. That's just the first time he stayed.

I'd seen him once before. I had assembled him out of a disaster to save me. I don't like remembering the real first time. But once I'm thinking about it, I can't help it.

The sound of screeching tires. I am alone and then, above me, I see him.

I reach up into a sky full of stars, George's white-gloved hand reaching down to me. Reaching up, up, our fingers touching—

"So it's weird how easily you let him go," Eleanor says. I shake off that other world.

"I didn't let him go," I say, confused.

"But you've been talking to Roberts. You've been co-operating. What do you think you're doing?"

The scorn on her face cuts me. The pain is strangely grounding. My stomach turns, recoiling from the fact of it, like a wound I've opened up, stitches splitting.

I haven't given him up yet, but I've given Roberts enough rope to hang me.

"You gave up pretty easily," Eleanor says, shaking her head.

"It wasn't easy at all. I've been here for almost a week."

"I thought you were the kind they'd have to torture." She runs her finger along the edge of one of her shark teeth. "Well, it doesn't really matter. You'd already lost him anyway."

Regret gnaws on my insides.

"What do you mean?"

"Have you been dreaming of George?"

"Of course not. It isn't safe."

"Right. Except, the thing is, even if you wanted to, I bet anything you couldn't. Not now. I tried to warn you. They steal your dreams here."

I roll my eyes.

"Metaphorically?"

"No. Literally."

"They *literally* steal dreams. And how exactly is that possible?"

"Just try it," Eleanor says. She raises her eyebrows in a challenge. "Try to go to George. Or bring him here . . . however you do it."

"What? No, I can't."

"Come on! Don't be shy."

"No, I mean . . . it's not like I can snap my fingers and do it."

"So how do you do it?"

"I just . . . let my mind wander."

"I want to see."

I don't like people to see, not when I'm really lost in George. I laugh, and I smile, and I move my hands and stuff. I move my lips without saying anything. But then I'll get knocked out of the dream and I'll be back in my room and so afraid that someone will catch me doing it.

I did get caught once back then. During recess, seventh grade, George and I were on an adventure. I thought I was being careful, but I must have been talking to myself. Some kids saw me.

"The *crazy* girl is talking to herself."

"We should get a teacher."

"No, she's like . . . damaged. My mom told me so."

"Yeah we're supposed to be nice to her. Just leave her alone."

That's what they whispered about me. They didn't think I heard them, but I did. "Don't listen," George told me. "You're not damaged." But it still hurt.

I told my mom about the kids making fun of me, thinking maybe I could just stay home forever. But all that happened was she called the school and I talked to a counselor. I didn't tell Mom exactly why I had been talking to myself, I just said I'd been playing. The counselor asked a lot of questions about knowing the difference between real and pretend, about hearing voices, and seeing things. I didn't even answer her after a while because I knew I was in trouble and I didn't want to get in more trouble, so I just shut down and said nothing. People who seem nice can be trying to trick you.

So she referred me for special education testing. I heard her on the phone even though I was in the hall. I wanted to say I was sorry, and that I shouldn't have said anything in the first place, and that I would be good and not weird anymore. George sat next to me in the office and told me to just stay quiet, it would all work out. I listened to him, and I didn't let my mask slip once.

My parents came to the school the next day and talked to someone and I didn't get tested and everything went back to normal.

I never got caught again.

But then, this is Eleanor.

She is staring at me expectantly.

"I don't know if I can do it if you're watching," I tell her.

"So I'll hide over here. You won't even notice me. Don't worry . . . I'll make sure no one sees you. You can have a nice little supervised visit with George," she says. "If you can find him, that is."

The thought is appealing: sitting with him for a while where I can see him. Asking him how I'm doing, if my ruse is working, and hearing him tell me that it's all going according to plan.

Without George, I feel like I can't think. Without my daydreams I feel slow and stupid and gray. I know what he would say, of course, but sometimes he surprises me. And with George, even if I know it already, to actually *feel* it is such a relief.

"And you'll tell me if anyone's coming?" I ask.

"You can trust me."

"Liar," I say, hoping it will sound brave and interesting. She winks at me, then settles in out of my line of sight.

I pretend she isn't there.

I let my eyes go loose on the real world.

I let my thoughts wander to George.

And I wait.

. . . I keep waiting.

The lines in the linoleum stay put, and the whir of machines and the air-conditioning do not evolve into grander stories.

Sometimes it takes a little more. A Portkey: one talisman of a story to get there in an instant. I think of George's gun in my hand, his white gloves, the camellias he gave me in Rio. I stand there holding each of these, locked solidly on my side of reality. And still no George.

I feel a little panicky. Sometimes I can set up the story by thinking my way up to it. "Once upon a time, there was a wizard named George who discovered that he was a prince." Or "The spy sat on the kitchen floor of the safe house stitching up his wounds." But when I walk to the door of my many fantasies, I find them all bricked up and barred.

The clock counts its seconds, and they pile up into minutes. Fifteen minutes. And all I can think of is the floor and the time.

Finally I do something I have never had to do. I try to conjure George.

I imagine his hair, charcoal and unruly. His pale skin like a Greek statue robbed of garish color by time. That suit: the Tom Ford O'Connor in effortless black. And his eyes. Blue as the sea after a storm, like Eleanor said. Where is Eleanor? Still watching. I force myself not to think of her before my conjured George starts to fall apart.

I look him over: it isn't right. This isn't George. This is a sad, half-formed thing, thin as a dream. He feels like a paper doll where once there was a boy. This is thinking *of* George. This isn't being with him. I abandon the golem and let it fall to dust.

"I can't do it," I say finally. "I don't understand."

"I told you," Eleanor says, emerging and glancing around the room. She looks at the tray from breakfast, gazes into the water, pokes the crusty dish. She examines a little cup that was once full of painkillers and looks at me knowingly.

"What's wrong with me? Why can't I   "

"Shhh. It's okay. You have to stay calm. They've already taken him from you."

"What?"

"I knew you weren't safe. I knew they'd do to you what they did to me."

"What did they do to you?"

"I can't go back. My spirits are gone. Yours are too."

"No . . . ," I say, horror rising sour in my throat. "No, that's not true. It's just that I didn't want to daydream while I was here, in case I got caught."

"Trust me, you *can't* anymore. They've already poisoned you. Soon it will be too late. Soon he'll be gone forever."

141

Forever? my mind echoes. It empties me of other thoughts.

No.

Never. I can't accept that.

When the curtain comes up on all of our daydreams, George is always right there to take a bow and start over again. George never really dies. How would that even be possible? I've asked him before and he never gives me a straight answer. But what happens to a thought when you are not thinking it?

He's not written down anywhere, not even in this journal. So, if I stopped thinking of him altogether, if I made myself forget, then he would really be gone. Thoughts are nothing if they go unremembered. They're electricity. But I think of George all the time, so his spark is never out, and he never dies. He is living lightning in my brain. We can die a thousand deaths in dreams and start over the next day.

But if I ever forget and let someone put out that spark . . . then he'd vanish. He'd never have existed, because there'd be no trace of him left.

"What can I do?" I ask. Eleanor shakes her head.

She wraps her arms around me and for the first time since I arrived, I really cry. I cry the way I used to in my room when it seemed like the world was ending and I felt so alone, before I lost even the energy to cry.

"How far are you willing to go?" she asks. And though I don't say it out loud, I know she has a secret that she wants to give up. A spy can sense these things. She knows something. She has already determined how far will get her home to her spirits. And I will have to make her tell me, whatever the cost, to get home to mine.

✳

Roberts is here but I'm not listening to her because I am panicked over George. *So good to see you wheeling yourself around these days. Isn't there anything you want to tell me? Blah, blah, blah, blah, such great progress.* I hear her like elevator music under my blinding panic. I keep saying the shortest thing possible because I really want to tell her to leave.

Finally she does and I wheel myself to the door and wait for the shark to arrive. I know she will come back as soon as the hallway clears. I watch. In the one still moment between parents and meds and checks and balloons, slippery as a villain, Eleanor makes her way down the hall to me. She's like George: unpredictable in a predictable way.

She's surprised to see me at the door.

"Are you going somewhere?" she asks. She sounds almost worried.

"No, I'm waiting for you."

"Good. Don't listen to what anyone out there says. They're all against us."

"Listen, I need to talk to you. About dreams."

She smiles a toothy smile under the toothy smile of her shark hood. "So you believe me now. See, I was a dreamer

143

too. That's what they said about me. Well, now I'm a schizo paranoid manic depressive whatever. But I used to live in a dream."

"Can I ask you something?" I say.

"Anything your heart desires. I speak only the truth."

"When you hallucinate, do you feel like you're hallucinating?"

"Is this about George?"

"Yes."

"You said he's not a hallucination."

"But can something *become* a hallucination?"

"Sure. I don't know. Why? Do you want him to be?"

I nod. "I have to see him. And I can't get to him."

"They poisoned you."

"I know. I believe you." I point to my untouched dinner.

Eleanor hesitates. For the first time, I see doubt in her eyes.

"What is it?" I ask.

"There is one way I know. . . ."

"How? Eleanor, I miss him. I need to see him."

"What a nice hallucination."

"He's not always nice."

"Hot."

"He gets angry sometimes," I confess. "I don't know how that's possible. I don't know what that means."

"My parents never get angry. It's because they don't care," she says.

I can remember the last time my parents really fought. That's what caused the crash. They were fighting because—

I shake my head and the thoughts evaporate.

"Does your boyfriend get angry?" I ask.

"Sure. We had one fight where he broke my finger. Then I put him through a window and that was the end of that."

I can imagine her in a beautiful dorm room, the way I imagine dorm rooms in boarding schools must look. Him stealing into her room and the fight they had. The way Eleanor smiles makes it so clear how much she loves him. The whole story of her life is in that smile. She looks at her hand like she loves the memory of it, how he fell out the window with a shocked little yelp.

"Imagination is a form of control," Eleanor says. "I read that in a book once. Fantasy is control and that's what makes it so satisfying."

"Sure. But it's only pretend."

"Don't you ever wonder if this isn't the real world? If this one is the dream?"

"Don't say that." I shiver and she laughs like crazy.

"Why, because you believe me?"

"No, because it makes me sad because it isn't true."

She cuddles up next to me. Her hair is ticklish.

"Do you trust me?"

"No."

"Well, nothing risked, nothing gained."

She hunts around in her shark costume, zipping and

unzipping pockets, digging deep into hidden layers. She reaches into the depths of her disguise and withdraws her fist, clenched tight. She holds it out to me.

I put my hand beneath hers. A tiny, nearly weightless thing drops into my palm. I look at it glinting there.

It is a razor wrapped safely in plastic.

"Some people call it cutting," she says, her eyes still on the blade. "But *cutting* is such a dirty word. I prefer to think of it as enlightenment."

My heart sinks. I look at her arms, with all their raised scars. Nausea wraps its dirty fingers around my stomach and climbs up my throat. Time slips off the clock and Eleanor becomes a series of slides, like in health class when they tell you not to do drugs. Slide one: just say no. Slide two: here's what happens if you don't.

I can't tell which slide we are on.

"Eleanor, I can't."

"It won't hurt. Not really. You just make the tiniest line. Do it when you're alone, somewhere no one can see. If they catch you they won't understand. If you want to get past the real, focused in like you've never been before, so thoroughly that you can see past the mundane and into that place we both know . . . this is how I get there. This is my door."

This is completely insane. I'm not one of "those girls." I don't hurt myself, make myself throw up, cut myself. Those girls belong in here, in psych wards. That's not me.

I hesitate. She runs her finger along the lines of her arm,

looking sad and a little ashamed. She says: "I just need to feel something sometimes, you know?"

I bite my lip, terror climbing my spine and telling me not to listen. But I can't help it, because I understand exactly what she means. And then I think of George and I don't care anymore.

I know it's stupid, and I know it's dangerous, but none of that matters because I just want to feel something.

I know what's coming for me. I'll go to Truman State, like everyone I'm in high school with. I'll have an okay job. I'll be someone's okay mom. I'll be Henry's okay wife if he doesn't get tired of me when Brother Raja takes off. I'll be okay. Everyone has always been okay.

And I want to be okay. But I also want to be with George. Because no matter what I do in my real life, it'll never be magical like it is with him. Because where does magic live in this world except in dreams? How many movies and how many books have I lost myself in, just to get away from one more day of silence and math homework and matching socks? The magic is in making something feel *real* for a moment. Because nothing in my life ever feels real.

I am lost in those thoughts, the way I sometimes get lost in daydreams. But it's worse when I get lost in reality, lost in sadness. When I'm dreaming, I'm happy. This other feeling, this black pool that sucks you under . . . I don't know what that is, but once you're drowning, you can't get out.

I just want to feel something more than okay. Okay?

The rest happens to some mechanical version of myself, and when I come to my senses, I am sitting in my room with a razor blade in my hand, and Eleanor is gone. I am all alone.

My mind is still for the first time since the crash. I think of the Star Palace and watch gardens bloom on all the walls of my hospital room: impossible vines and flowers out of season inviting me home. I get out of bed, but when I turn around, I am still there in bed with my broken leg. I start to worry, looking at her, looking at me. She is pathetic: a shell holding me back.

"What's wrong with you?" I ask her.

She holds up her hand and she's got the razor blade. She drops it on the sheets. She looks at me, horrified, like I am the one who is too pathetic to keep to my promises, to seek and find. She starts screaming, and it is like listening to her from the bottom of the ocean.

I am light-headed. I look down and my own hands are dripping with blood. But I look at her and she's not bleeding, she's just looking at me with her mouth agape. She's fine. She barely even cut herself. That tiny red line is nothing among the scrapes from the crash. It's me, this imaginary me, who is bleeding to death. *Is this real?* I think. I know it's not. I know I'm dreaming somehow, and I don't know how to handle that.

The real me is screaming. The imaginary me is tethered

to her. And we're all going down as nurses swarm into our room, pouring over us like a storm.

But then George comes to save me like he always does. "I've missed you," he says, and I don't say anything. I am already kissing him, already gone.

A PLACE TO HIDE

Sadie's dresser was covered in books, as was every horizontal surface in her room. It left little space for anything else. Recently her books had been taken over by the slowly creeping growth of her mom's discarded makeup. The collection expanded like an invasive species, rendering *Frankenstein* and *Wuthering Heights*—her summer reading before junior year—inaccessible without toppling lipstick and nail polish all over the floor.

"Look at you," George sneered as Sadie attempted to apply liquid eyeliner for the third time. Her hands were shaking, and yet again, she ruptured the clean swoop of a cat eye, resulting in a knobby goth mess.

George sighed and shoved his hands into his pockets, pacing behind her. He began whistling a familiar tune, but she ignored him. He peevishly continued until finally, under his breath, he began to sing:

"There is no life I know to compare with pure imagination—"

"You're distracting me, George," Sadie snapped, glaring at him in the cabinet mirror. From the corner of her eye, she could see him pouting, but she focused on herself and tried to salvage her boring face. She blurred the black liner into two dark pockets over her eyes and smeared glitter on her eyelids, but gave up on the whole concept of blush and lipstick. She had a kind of ghoulish look that she hoped Henry would like. She looked like the rest of his band, at least. She had wanted to ask Lucie what to wear to the concert, what to wear to impress Henry, but she'd been too embarrassed. She didn't want Lucie to know, but Sadie was certain: something was wrong between her and Henry.

"You better not tell her," George said. "Lucie's so pretty, and she's got so much in common with Henry."

"What does that mean?"

"You know what it means. If you ask me, you look ridiculous. In case you're wondering."

"Why are you being this way?"

"Because I'm jealous," he muttered. It was hard to tell if he was serious. He lit a cigarette and took a sip of his old-fashioned. She loved the way it smelled. He was trying to distract her.

"I have to go," she said.

"Don't go."

"Why?"

George set the glass down hard on the desk, spilling whiskey all over a colony of Penguin Classics.

"Because no matter what you think you have with him, he'll never be me."

Sadie slammed the cabinet door, but when she turned to face him, he was gone.

✳

It seemed to Sadie a dreadful lie to call the City Museum a museum. It was chaotic. Nothing lived in frames, and nothing was labeled. It was loud. One always needed to look out for children running, or dragons, or any other manner of demon. It did not leave space to think. It did not leave space for George.

But it was Henry's favorite place, so Sadie was happy to be there. It was beautiful like a collage: all the pieces of different times and places repurposed into something truly different. Artists had salvaged a city and built a fantasy. Painted factory rollers lined up into slides and concrete curled into caves. Everything was wild and unusual there: a circus indoors, a machine to make shoelaces. Mrs. Vaughn had said it was the perfect place for his band to play because it defied description, just like Brother Raja, and Henry had blushed with pride despite himself.

As Henry reminded his mom, they were only the opening act, so it wasn't that big of a deal. He measured himself against gods and legends. For mere mortals, it was quite a big deal. The *Riverfront Times* had branded Brother Raja a band to watch and recommended that parents "give a second listen to the poorly dressed teens playing folk rock disco disguised as punk." Their T-shirts with the elephant logo printed right in Henry's backyard were showing up not only around Webster, but on staff at Vintage Vinyl and around the WashU campus. *Precocious* was the adjective everyone used for Henry. *Raw* was what they called Lucie. As the review had said: "These high school punks are showing us that the suburbs are alive with the sound of music."

The show didn't start for a few hours. Henry was already nervous, his hand warm and damp in her own, as they strolled through the concrete caves. His black eyeliner and all-black clothes drew a few parental stares from the adults tethered to toddlers, but his smile softened every hard brow. Even dressed like the devil, he still looked like a nice boy.

Sadie watched the covetous stares of Henry's blossoming fan club. To girls from local schools he was no longer invisible, if he ever had been. When Henry waved, they screamed, turned bright red, and vanished. He just looked confused.

"But *you're* not confused," George whispered. "You know exactly what's going on."

*

"Are you excited?" Sadie asked to break the silence. Her knees were curled up underneath her in a hidden pocket they had found. It was a dragon's den just big enough for the two of them. Sadie could smell Henry's shampoo: something flowery he'd taken from his mom, totally at odds with his desperately authentic punk look.

"Yeah, it's gonna be a good show," Henry said, fidgeting with his shoelaces. "I'm happy you're here."

"I mean about everything. How everything's ... happening," she said. Henry shrugged.

"Sure. It's nice to have an audience." He hesitated. "But I miss ... you know. The way things used to be."

"What do you mean?"

He shrugged again. He could be so hesitant to say anything these days. He was so busy all the time with the band and lessons and applying for college that they mostly texted anyway. In some ways, she liked it. When they were together, it was like there was a wall casting a shadow over them. Not between them, but in front of them. She felt awkward, like she was being left behind and she didn't know how to follow.

"Nothing," he said finally, touching her with the squeaky toe of his all-black Converse. "I just miss ... having fun doing nothing. Matinees. Reading on the porch." He fidgeted with the friendship bracelet Sadie had made him. It was old, nearly falling apart. She reflexively touched her own.

"Me too," Sadie said. And she did miss how it had been then. But it wasn't like she would have wanted to go back either. It was confusing. She felt herself retreating into her thoughts, puzzling it out. What did she want? George would know.

"Are you . . . ?" she began, but then she wasn't sure what question to ask.

"What?"

"Nothing."

"You can ask me anything."

"I just want you to be happy."

"That's not a question," Henry said.

"I'm sorry." Sadie was too afraid of the answers to her questions to even ask them.

The awkwardness settled into the cave with them, so they climbed out and wandered toward food. They weren't hungry, but it was something to do. The whole band had made it, according to the massive group text they all shared. Sadie spotted a few of them: Lucie was standing in line for a hot dog, chatting with her other friends. She had a whole pack that followed her everywhere. She caught Sadie's eye and made a face, waving. Sadie smiled and nodded. In the distance, she glimpsed George. He was wearing his robes and he had his wand out, a dragon crawling around his feet, affectionate as a puppy. She'd been thinking of dragons ever since they'd come in. Dragons were fascinating. George beckoned to her urgently, looked over his shoulder as though he was being chased. He ran out of sight and Sadie—

"Sadie? Sadie!"

"What?" Sadie asked, suddenly aware that Henry had been calling her name for some time.

"I asked you something."

"What was it?"

"Weren't you paying attention?"

"Yeah, it's just loud in here."

"Come on. You weren't even listening. You were just staring into space."

"I wasn't. I can barely hear you now. Don't be mad."

"I can't help it!" he snapped. "It's like, no matter where we are, you're always looking somewhere else. I can never get to where you are."

"But I'm right here!" Sadie pleaded.

"Who are you thinking about?" he asked. "You're always smiling when you're far away. But you never smile when you're with me. Not really."

"That's not true. I didn't hear you. What did you ask me?"

"I asked if you love me."

Sadie's voice caught in her throat. She didn't know what to say. She looked back to where Lucie had been standing, and thankfully Lucie was looking right at her. Always on cue, Lucie jogged over.

"What's up?" Lucie asked.

"Where have you been?" Henry snapped.

"Checking our gear, unlike some slackers." Lucie poked him in the ribs. Henry batted her back, and suddenly they were play-wrestling.

"Isn't that cute?" George whispered in Sadie's ear. Sadie shook her head as hard as she could and he vanished.

"What are you doing, Sadie?" Lucie asked, grabbing her. Lucie held her so tight she couldn't move, stopping her from shaking. Sadie hated to be held down, it made her feel strapped in, out of control.

"Nothing!" she shouted in embarrassment as she wrenched herself away. Henry and Lucie looked at each other, having the same kind of secret conversation Sadie's parents always had.

"I'm fine," Sadie said. If Henry left her for Lucie, maybe they'd still be friends. And then she wouldn't have to worry anymore about it all falling apart.

But when Sadie thought about it, she knew it wouldn't happen like that. Lucie wouldn't do that. Neither would Henry. What was she thinking?

"Okay. Jeez! You're being so weird," Lucie said after a minute. *Weird* stung, but Sadie knew she deserved it. She felt weird. "Let's get hot dogs." Lucie's voice was the comforting purr of an engine capable of handling anything the road would throw at her. She was always on to the next thing, unbreakable.

"How can you eat before a show?" asked Henry.

"Running. Constantly. We're going to win. At running. Which is a sport. According to your mom."

"Thank you, Lucie, for the information. You truly are a gift to humanity."

"That's what your mom said last night," said Lucie.

Sadie laughed. Lucie always made her smile. Henry glared at them and they both stopped. "Oh, lighten up. What's the matter with you two?" Lucie asked.

"It's nothing," Sadie said, looking at the floor.

Lucie cleared her throat and punched Henry hard on the shoulder. He yelped. "Stop being a psycho," she commanded. And when Lucie commanded anyone, they obeyed. Lucie was always in control. Sadie envied that.

They didn't say anything else, not in front of Lucie, and not to each other. But Sadie couldn't stop thinking about it. When the show started and Henry went onstage, she thought: it wasn't fair. When he was onstage he couldn't think about anything but music. It consumed him. He was furious, but at that moment Sadie was certain that he didn't feel anything but music. He went away to his other world, and she was in the audience suffering alone.

Staring up at him, watching him so close but so far away in his head, Sadie missed him.

She loved him. She really did.

But then, there was always George.

*

After the show, Henry smelled like sweat and smoke from the fire pit. His Honda was stuffed to its breaking point with musical instruments and gear. It sagged on its wheels. Sadie could hear the high-pitched song of its dying serpentine belt. She'd been helping out at the shop with her parents more and more, and everywhere she turned she saw mechanisms in need of repair. She had a knack for it.

Henry whooped, still high from being on the stage, as the stereo shifted from some abstract guitar torture to a more recognizable White Stripes throwback.

Sadie sat in the passenger's seat with a misplaced tambourine in her lap, smiling.

"Can we drop this stuff off at my house before I take you home?" Henry asked, running his hand through his sweaty hair. Sadie nodded. They went over a speed bump and the tambourine rattled in her lap.

"Those are called sleeping policemen in England," she announced. She was nervous for some reason, spewing facts.

"Really? That's hilarious," Henry said. "I love how you know everything. When I take you to England, we'll know what to call them. You can be our guide."

Sadie offered a limp smile. Henry sang, beating the steering wheel into submission with a drum solo.

They pulled into the driveway with a mechanical whine and a crunch and sat in silence for a few breaths. Henry stared at the garage door, watching it rise at the behest of the groaning motor.

"My mom's not home," Henry said. He leaned over quickly and kissed her. "She's on a date with Mr. Rigley." Sadie recoiled.

"Like, gym Nazi Mr. Rigley?"

"Yeah," Henry said. "She's been dating him for a few weeks. Don't tell anyone."

Sadie's heart sank. Mrs. Vaughn seemed so untouchable, like a queen. It was hard to imagine her dating anyone, let alone a universally loathed gym teacher.

"What does she see in him?" Sadie asked.

"Same thing she saw in my dad, I guess," Henry said. "A hero."

Sadie understood that. Henry's nearly imaginary army father was a man of stories and legends, but he didn't sound like a match for the sparkling, bookish, manic Mrs. Vaughn that Sadie knew. Henry's dad was a statue, a portrait in uniform. Not to Henry, of course, but from a distance he looked like a page out of a history book. Henry always said those first years moving around military bases were what broke up his parents, but Sadie wondered if it wasn't just the disappointment of a hero stepping off the page. No one from that two-dimensional world of text could ever survive three dimensions.

They unloaded the band's equipment into the converted garage, hurrying to beat the rain. A big sheet with the elephant logo hung over an arsenal of disused tools glimmering in the falling light. Thunder broke overhead so loud that the drum kit shook. It began to pour.

"Come inside for a second. Maybe it'll slow down," Henry said as the garage closed. He shook the water from his hair and made cute little noises of exertion. Sadie followed him into the familiar living room. Pictures of Henry's band and some of Sadie had joined the pillage of history spanning the walls. Sadie and Henry going to the winter formal. Sadie and Henry asleep in the hammock. Sadie and Lucie after a race, lying in the grass. Brother Raja and Sadie eating pizza in the garage, slices raised to salute Mrs. Vaughn behind the camera. Sadie's favorite was a picture of herself, Henry, and Lucie on the floor watching a movie, so absorbed they hadn't noticed the camera. Their eyes were wide and their faces were lit up with the eerie gray of the television. All around them was darkness, but they were so bright.

Little moments, among the toils of Shackleton, the foxholes, the mountaintops. Little victories next to the highest peaks, the greatest depths, the firsts and the finals. Mrs. Vaughn called it her wall of heroes.

Henry had disappeared while she was distracted with the pictures. Sadie went into the kitchen, grabbed a Diet Coke from the fridge, and poured it into a glass from the dishwasher, where their dishes always lived. She hung her damp bag in the mudroom. In the living room, she sat carefully on the wobbly ottoman, staring into the black TV screen at her reflection. She was wet and cold.

Behind her in the screen, she saw George's lean reflection, no more than a silhouette. He looked angry and sad.

"Sorry, did I scare you?" Henry asked when she whipped around. He had a bottle of whiskey in one hand and a pack of cigarettes in the other.

"A little," Sadie said. She turned back to the screen. It had been Henry all along.

"Celebration?" Henry asked. "My dad bought all this for me the last time I went to see him. We went out all night in

Tokyo and no one even stopped me when we went into bars. He called it learning sin to overcome sin. It's like a macho family thing. His dad did it and his dad before him. . . ."

"Your dad bought you alcohol?" Henry had gone to Japan for two weeks that summer, texting her every day. He hadn't said anything about nights on the town. Every picture had been anime and temples and Harajuku Girls. He'd mentioned they'd had some man-to-man talks, whatever those were. His dad was the one thing Henry kept secret, outside of veneration in swashbuckling anecdotes. Henry with his dad was an alternate universe Sadie couldn't even imagine.

"He drank it with me. He made me swear I would drink it at home and that I wouldn't drive. It's supposed to be really good Japanese whiskey. I wanted to surprise you."

"And your mom lets you drink in your room?"

"She doesn't know," he said with a grin. Sadie doubted that. Nothing got by Mrs. Vaughn: not a spelling mistake in class, not a missed practice for cross-country. Sadie's hair was dripping onto the floor. She wondered what Mrs. Vaughn would deduce from that and reminded herself to wipe it up before she left.

"How will you drive me home if we drink it?" Sadie asked. Henry reached out and put his arms over her shoulders. She could feel the heavy bottle on her back.

"I was thinking maybe . . . would it be okay if I didn't? My mom is gone for the night."

Sadie blushed.

"I don't mean . . . ," Henry trailed off, pulling away. "I mean, we don't have to . . ."

He sighed. "I just want to spend time with you. I miss you. Don't you ever miss me?"

She stared at him for a long time, standing there with a bottle of whiskey and cigarettes, all of him soaking wet. His black shirt was dripping. His eyeliner made him look like he'd been crying. Sadie's heart beat hard in her chest, pounding against the moment of a decision. She could feel the vibrations in the track, standing at a crossroads between two out-of-control trains. She felt like the girl tied to the track between them.

"Yes, I miss you," Sadie said. She took the bottle and poured two glasses, neat, handing one to Henry.

"Na zdorovie," she said, clinking his glass. He took a sip and winced. Sadie took a gulp and choked, dribbling her drink on the floor. Henry laughed.

"It's an acquired taste," he said.

Sadie thought of all the dream cocktails she'd drunk, all the sips stolen from George. This did not live up to those drinks. It was horrible. Nothing dignified, woody, or rich about it. Just burning and choking. Real whiskey was nothing like what she'd read about.

When she looked at Henry, he was still laughing, but catching her eye, he stopped.

"What is it?" she asked.

"You have the bluest eyes of any girl in the world. When you look at me, it's like I can't look away."

163

Sadie woke with a gasp. Her vision was spinning, careening painfully. She grabbed her phone. It was one in the morning. She'd barely dozed off.

She pulled the grimy covers up under her chin. They smelled like sweat. They smelled like clean laundry under which dirty laundry was hiding: like Febreze couldn't quite get out the smell.

Henry lay next to her, sleeping. His chest rose and fell, his ripped T-shirt hanging open to reveal a few random long hairs.

Sadie extracted herself from the bed with surgical precision. Henry stirred, awakened by her movement.

"Are you leaving?" he whispered.

"Your mom will be home," she whispered back.

"No, she's out for the night. She's staying at her boyfriend's house. I promise."

"Well, my parents are home," Sadie countered. He put his hand on her arm.

"Hey," he said. The bottle of whiskey had fallen over and she could see the remaining droplets congregating in one corner. Even thinking of it turned her stomach. The muddy remains of the tea-light candles had gone out, and his iPhone had died. The speakers it was attached to continued to buzz. A square foil wrapper sat crumpled in a ball on top of the piles of CDs that covered his bedside table.

She looked at him, hoping to get lost in his eyes. His eyes

were so black that he looked like a deer. There was nothing to get lost in, just darkness.

"Hey," he said again, and she managed to focus. It wasn't like in a movie or a book, him lying there. He didn't look cool. He looked confused. His faux 'hawk was all mussed across his head, and he had glitter on half his face from her makeup and the concert. She was smeared all over him.

"Hey," she said back finally.

They sat awkwardly in the silence for a minute. Then he kissed her. His kisses tasted like sour ash after half a cigarette. It didn't smell wonderful and sophisticated like George's cigarettes. It was nothing like how she had imagined it. The stench lingered in the air and deep in Henry's throat. How could smoking taste so bad?

She stood up. She felt nauseous and unsteady, but she put her hair back coolly, focusing on containing everything in one controlled little knot.

"Was it okay?" His hand brushed her leg. Everything was perfect. What was wrong with her?

"Yeah," she said after a moment, stepping away from him. "I just have to go. My parents are home."

"Can't you stay the night?"

"No." She wanted to hold him. She wanted to run away. Everything was a muddle.

"We have ice cream," he said desperately.

"I have to go," she said. Her heart was pounding so hard that she was shaking. "I'll see you tomorrow."

"Can I walk you home?"

"No, I'll be fine," Sadie said.

She grabbed her bag, and she went to the door. She hesitated, and she went back, and she kissed his wonderful bewildered face one more time, missing his mouth entirely. Then she marched through the house and out his so-familiar front door into the night. And then she could finally breathe.

✳

The street was cool and empty, glittering with the memory of rain.

Sadie walked slowly, her bag digging into her shoulder. She felt sore and damp and uncomfortable. She felt disgusting. She wished it would start raining again so she would feel clean.

"We could go to the Star Palace," George said, walking beside her.

"Not now." She felt sick.

"Come on, Sadie." He started walking backward in front of her. She looked at him, and he was so gleeful she wanted to hit him.

"Now, now. Real's not much fun, is it?" he teased. She watched the pavement pass by and her feet come into view, one after the other. In the corner of her vision George's shiny black shoes kept distracting her.

"I'm sorry. Cheer up, darling. I just missed you. That's

all. I know you'll go your own way eventually. I just thought we'd have more time."

"Go away, George," Sadie said, and he vanished.

She focused on walking. She counted her steps: one two, one two. Against her will she watched the scene unfold with Henry over and over in her mind. Her head hurt from drinking. She couldn't quite get it clear. But then it had all been over so quickly, so strangely.

She imagined Henry's face, and her heart filled with the kind of ache she'd dreamed of: wanting to touch him, wanting to be near him. He kept her in the present like an anchor. How could he be any more perfect? She didn't deserve him. He was a rock star grown out of books.

So why did she feel so awful?

She wiped her face clean, which only managed to further streak her eyeliner. She straightened out her clothes, but there was no salvaging it. There was no way to make herself look put together.

She walked slowly up the driveway, in no hurry to get home. She passed George sitting solemnly on the front step tossing pebbles into the air and letting them fall to the earth. She didn't even look at him.

"You're home late," her mom said as Sadie came inside.

"I texted you asking if I could stay out," Sadie said, hovering near the door so her parents couldn't smell the reek of alcohol and cigarettes and whatever other sins were emanating off her.

"Yeah, and when the answer to the text is no, you're supposed to come home," her mom replied, an obvious glimmer of suspicion crossing her face.

Her parents were in the kitchen, her dad staring intently into a battered old four-slot toaster without a spark of life left in it. Her mom was changing the record, inspecting album covers. They'd been listening to a lot of classical music, nerding out about this or that concerto. They even went to the symphony sometimes. Sadie could barely tell all the songs apart.

"Henry dropped me off," Sadie said, kicking off her shoes.

Her dad looked at his watch. "It's two in the morning," he said.

"The show went late. Really late."

Her parents exchanged a glance. Sadie realized: they never stayed up this late. They'd been waiting.

"I'm sorry," she said. "I just . . . it was important. To Henry. It was a big deal."

"Okay, well, next time not so late," her mom said. "How was it?"

"What?"

"Henry's show. How was it?"

"It was . . . perfect," Sadie replied.

Her parents smiled. Her dad went back to his toaster and her mom changed the record. The speakers swept into a waltz. Their massive speaker system filled the whole house with music. She'd be able to hear it even in the basement.

Sadie felt her phone vibrate and she looked at it. It was a text from Henry. "I love you," it said. She put her phone back into her pocket and marched toward the back door.

"Sadie?" her mom called after her.

"Where are you going?" her dad asked.

"Outside for some air," she mumbled.

"It's two in the morning," her mom said.

"I'm just going out back."

She let the screen door slam behind her. She ran barefoot out to Old Charlotte, yanked open her door, and closed herself in.

It didn't feel like another world inside like it usually did.

It felt like a violated world, a broken one.

Henry always felt like he was a step behind, but Sadie knew that she was the one running to catch up. Tomorrow she would be happy. Tomorrow she would text him that she loved him. Tomorrow, and tomorrow, and tomorrow, she would kiss him and touch him and be touched by him. But tonight she was lost.

The backseat was cold and empty and there was nothing for her to blow her nose on. She tried to stop crying, tried focusing on anything else. A spell. A palace. A mystery. Anything. An old favorite: just a hand to hold. Anything. Anything but this emptiness.

"Don't cry," George said. As though she were under one of his magic spells, she found that she had stopped. The night grew completely quiet. Nothing existed outside Old Charlotte's foggy windows.

George leaned in hesitantly, as though she still had the power to stop him. His face was almost touching hers, electric. He took shallow nervous breaths, and she could feel each one light up the space between them with static begging to connect skin to skin, lips to lips. She stayed perfectly still staring into his blue eyes. Destiny, gravity, force. Something brought them together. His lips were soft but not wet, his skin smooth and dry.

"Did you like it?" he asked when he pulled away. She nodded. She turned away from him, and he pulled her face toward his and kissed her again. He leaned in close to whisper in her ear.

"The untold want—"

"I don't need poetry," Sadie said, searching those eyes for an answer. "I just need you."

And then she kissed him back. She kissed him hard. Not sloppy and wet and fumbling as before, but confident. It was like they could read each other's minds. His arms wrapped around her and hers found their way around his neck, and she felt the same things she had felt before: the strange automatic motion of him, manifested into something more. His fingers laced their way easily around buttons, and his hand took its place on her back, tempting her toward him. He lifted her up and suddenly she was on top of him—

Just then Sadie heard a door slam and the whole thing vanished in a wave of panic. She peeked out the window. No one was there, and all the lights had gone off. Her parents had gone to bed. It was dark, and she was alone. Completely alone.

She leaned back in the truck and lay down in the seat, putting her earbuds in. Her jeans had bunched themselves up in a strange way and she reached down to the sore wetness that remained of Henry, her only recollection of the main event warped by this disgusting mess it had made and the smell he'd left on her.

Sadie let her hands feel that hard seam of her jeans that held everything together, zipping her in. It divided her in two. She leaned back into the seat and listened to the music from her phone, all the old songs she used to love. A loose spring was sharp against her shoulder. It grounded her. She put her bare feet on the old hand crank of the window, where they fit perfectly. As she pulled at the seam, she imagined how it might have been with George, and what his hands would have felt like, and how magic and different it all could have been and never would be.

Something was over and something had started with Henry. And she cried, because it had felt strange, and it had felt right, but nothing had been magical at all.

DAY 8

I sit up bolt-straight, sweating. A nightmare. The sudden movement hurts everything inside me all at once: my broken leg, my horrible knotty stitches, and all the wounds that no one can see.

My dreams have become no more than harsher and harsher elaborations on my days here. I close my eyes in the hospital, and dream of the hospital, and wake up in the hospital. There's no escape.

I was supposed to go home two days ago.

I haven't been alone since the second that razor hit my skin. There are eyes on me all the time. In a way I'm glad. I'm afraid.

I don't know who that person was who cut herself. I mean, it was me, but it was like watching a movie. Even now I feel like a shadow watching myself.

I look at my leg and try to settle down, but my thoughts are like a hurricane. It still doesn't seem real. I touch the tiny cut. It feels far away.

I'm so tired and so anxious.

My parents are completely freaked out, and I can't even be upset with them because who wouldn't be? I'm terrified that everyone at school is going to find out and think I'm like suicidal or something.

I told Dr. Roberts that it was an accident. I said it over and over, but even I can't explain this one away. I mean, how could I? There's no lie I can tell that would explain how cutting myself with a razor I wasn't even supposed to have was an accident. What I want to say is "It wasn't me," because it wasn't, in a way. But I can't explain that either.

I keep replaying it in my head.

"We're very concerned," Dr. Roberts said once they got me all cleaned up. "Where did you get that razor blade?"

I could still hear the nurses shouting and everyone yelling and everything just felt like noise. I just shook my head. My default setting is silence. Tell no one anything and you're always safe from what they might think. You never know what you might give away by accident.

"Did Eleanor give it to you?" Dr. Roberts asked.

I thought yes and said no. Eleanor trusted me. But I've been drifting, drifting away. I can't remember, having repeated the story to myself so many times, if I said yes or no. I fear I've betrayed yet another friend.

If I betray them all, I'll be alone forever.

And that is exactly what I deserve.

✳

I've had months that felt like this before: I fade in and out of sleep, all day long. Sometimes I don't even get out of bed except to put on a show for the world. If you don't put your mask on, you endure one afternoon a week with a psychiatrist. That's the deal. So I get up and perform when I have to, because that's what keeps George safe. Even when I want nothing more than to sleep, I make sure no one can see how empty I am inside.

What do I care now? I'm already in a hospital. I might as well sleep. I could sleep forever.

But today I open my eyes and Henry is standing in the doorway, leaning there in his Levi's jacket with all the patches from all the bands I had to look up on the Internet. I smile. But he is so still, like a ghost watching over me, and I fall back asleep because I'm dreaming, I think, and it is so strange to be dreaming at all, let alone dreaming of him.

When I wake up again, he's next to my bed reading. I open my eyes and it takes so long for him to notice me. I can see that it is taking all of his strength to look at the book and not at me, like he is counting the seconds until he can check on me again. When our eyes meet he comes alive.

"Hey, stranger," he says. He puts his hand on my hand. I don't say anything. God, what could I have said in my sleep? My heart starts to flutter.

"I wanted to come sooner, but they said you were too sick. And then I called and you—"

"It was just a misunderstanding," I say.

"Your parents said I could come. I would have come anyway, but I did ask."

"You didn't have to ask."

"I wanted to make sure you weren't too . . . that you wanted to see me," he says. "I've been thinking of you. Every day."

"I've been thinking of you too. Thank you for the iPod."

"Did you like the music? There's a song on there I wrote for you."

"I love it. It'll be better when you can play it for me yourself."

"It kills onstage. I can't wait for you to be there."

The conversation stops, and he starts gearing up to ask me something hard, so I have to keep talking.

"Are you here alone?" I ask.

"Your parents are down in the cafeteria."

"But you didn't bring Lucie?" I kind of hoped we'd have a buffer so he couldn't ask me anything too crazy.

"Oh . . . ," he starts, looking a little hurt. "No, I thought it could be just us today. I mean, I haven't seen you in so long."

"Okay," I say. "That'll be nice."

"Okay," he says. We stare at each other for a long time, like we used to at the library when we were just kids. I can tell he wants to ask me about the crash, and I watch as he decides not to.

Instead he leans over and kisses me.

He loves honesty. But he's figuring out the art of secrets. Maybe he knew how to live with secrets all along.

All of a sudden I have a strange feeling that I don't know him at all: that there are whole secret worlds inside him, just like I have a universe inside me. *Henry has secrets,* I realize.

What if they have to do with me?

✳

Over lunch, we talk about the people we know and what is going on at home. Henry's been on the road, and he's brought me all kinds of little things from across the Midwest to prove that he's been thinking of me. A tiny stuffed buffalo. One of those weird collectible tiny spoons. Stickers and patches and magnets he saved in a Ziploc bag.

"My mom says next year when we go on tour you should come with us. She said I did nothing but whine about you when I called home. She kept saying, 'Suck it up, soldier,' and telling me about all these old battles I don't care about."

I smile. "That sounds like your mom."

"Yeah. She thought your parents would be okay with it next year, and anyway, you'll be almost in college, and then you could share a room with Lucie and it'd all work out."

"Can I ask you something?"

"Of course."

"Does your mom think there's something wrong with me? Is that why she's nice to me? Because she feels bad?"

"No," Henry says, but his face is all dark the way it gets

when he lies. He doesn't do it often or well, so I remember the look. "No, she doesn't think anything is wrong with you. But she worries," he admits after a moment.

"About what?" He doesn't want to say anything but I wait him out.

"Because you're so different. You're special," he lies. "I mean, she's a teacher and my mom. So she worries."

"How am I different?"

"Sadie . . ."

"No, how?"

He sighs.

"Well, you like to be alone."

"So?"

He rolls his eyes.

"Fine. You really want to know? We used to see you . . . like, walking around. We'd see you walking around with an old Walkman and a ratty old briefcase. Or on the swings by yourself. We'd drive by in one direction and we'd come back and you'd still be there. And that was a long time ago, before I really knew you. And my mom would wonder if you were okay. But that's it. She doesn't think anything is wrong with you. How would she know, anyway?"

"She wouldn't," I say, maybe too sharp.

"Except . . ."

He pauses. He can't look at me.

"Except what?"

"Once she called your parents and they talked for a long time," he admits.

"What?"

"It's not a big deal."

"Are you kidding? That is . . ." I'm just speechless. A betrayal? Mortifying? I can't imagine anything worse than my boyfriend's mom calling my parents to talk about all the things wrong with me. How could anything be worse?

"I don't know what they said," Henry says, as though this will comfort me.

"When was this?"

"A few months ago. Right before I left."

"Why didn't you tell me?"

"I just . . ."

"Why wouldn't you tell me something like that?"

"Because I'm the one who asked her to!" he says. And suddenly the whole thing shifts into focus and I understand and it is so bad I can't even process it. My whole brain shuts down.

"I'm sorry," he says. "Come on, Sadie. Anyone would worry. You seemed so—"

"No one needs to worry about me," I say.

He sighs and shrugs: as you wish. He looks just like his mom when he does it.

"Are we okay?" he asks. I can hear that he's sorry. But I am so angry. You know what he is? Controlling. He always has been. He says he's worried and he wants to take care of me, but I don't need him to, and . . .

And what? Why am I so mad?

I try my best to bury my anger deep, but there's no room left for it. It is a shallow grave, a pit full of the bones of hurts I've suffocated inside myself.

"So what's the damage on your leg?" he asks, changing the subject.

"Nothing!" I say too quickly, my guard up. He looks perplexed and I realize he's talking about the obvious damage. Not the cut. Not the future scar, the reminder of Eleanor. "It's broken. But it'll be fine. It's *already* fine. They're holding me here for some stupid misunderstanding."

"I want you to get well," he says, as though wanting it will do anything.

"I want to go home."

And I realize how true it is. Then the tears are coming and I can't stop them.

"Baby—"

"No, I want to get out of here. You don't get it. This place is awful. They think . . ."

I cover my mouth to stop the secrets.

"What do they think?"

"Nothing, I just need to go home."

Henry sighs. He stands up and paces the room, looking out the window, out the door.

"Listen, I know this is hard—"

"No, you don't know anything! You never do. You think I'm crazy, but they're holding me hostage and trying to . . . to change me."

"Change you?"

"Turn me into a different person. They think something is wrong with me, just like everyone else."

"Maybe . . ."

"Maybe what? Maybe they're right?"

"I didn't say that."

"You thought it. I can see it on your face. God, I just want to go home."

Henry sighs, gears turning, calculations pending.

"*Is* that what you want?" he asks.

"Yes."

"Are you sure?"

"Yes."

"Come on," he says, grabbing my wheelchair. "I can get you in the car if we put down the backseat."

"What?"

"My mom will kill me. But a real hero will face certain demise for the people he loves. That's what my dad says. Probably not quite what he meant."

＊

Henry pushes my wheelchair out into the hall. The nurses at their desk smile at us as we pass by.

"Here's the young man who's been calling you, Sadie," says the nurse whose name I really should remember. I blush.

"Guilty as charged," Henry says. "We were just going to step out for a second."

"Uh, no. Nice try, young man," says the nurse. "I'm afraid that's not allowed."

"Miss . . . it's only that we haven't seen each other for so long, and—"

"Then wheel your adorable selves down to the community room and watch TV," she says. "It's right down the hall."

"Absolutely," Henry says, eyeing the door. "Sounds wonderful."

Henry pushes the wheelchair back toward my room and sighs. We look back at the door but catch the eye of the nurse.

"Well, that's a bust," I say.

"We've barely started, sugar. Don't give up yet," he says. He sniffs the air.

"What is it?"

"Smoke," he says with a grin. "You can smell it on their clothes. You know nurses."

George's cigarettes smell and taste nothing like real cigarettes, so sometimes I forget that the nasty smell he's talking about is from smoking. The one time Henry and I tried smoking, I found out the hard way how much it sucks.

But he's right. Even under that weird antiseptic smell, it's there. You can never get it off. Double gross.

I say: "You don't think . . ."

"Yes, I do. I bet there's a back door somewhere in here."

We wheel our way through the common room. There, we navigate a maze of girls I haven't seen before. I haven't left my room, so I don't really know who is here. Some of the girls are young, some are older. Some are in bandages, others are rail-thin, others are staring into space. Some are with their parents. Some are laughing and sitting together like they're in a cafeteria. I can't help but notice that Eleanor isn't among them, and I'm so disappointed.

I raged against group therapy because I wasn't sick. Now I'm horrified at the idea. Are these my peers?

We look down the halls leading out. A nurse is sitting guard over the room, but she is distracted by someone on the floor crying as though her world were ending. Henry shudders. I can feel him behind me.

"I can't believe they locked you up in here."

"Me neither," I say, staring at a girl my own age making friendship bracelets with some string tied around one of her toes. She is smiling and waves at me. She looks tired but normal. What could be wrong with her, that you can't even see it?

We escape into the hall while the nurse is distracted.

"There!" Henry points to a door propped open with a coffee can. We rush toward it and, before anyone notices, we are out of the cold light of the building and into the warm sun.

✳

The air is thick. I forgot that it's July. Hot weather always makes me confused.

It is a fire escape or something. Five stories up. There is no way I am going to make it down on my own. Henry sighs.

"I feel like you usually have a quote by some dead explorer in these situations," he says.

"I can't think of one."

"Really?"

I search my mind, but nothing seems apt, and I still feel cloudy.

"Maybe this is unprecedented," I say. "I've never been on a fire escape in a wheelchair before."

"We're pioneers, then," he says, leaning way too far over the edge.

"If only these wheels were wings," I say.

"There you go! Perfect. Now you just have to remember it for your memoirs." It is kind of perfect, actually, for our dilemma. I feel momentarily clever, and a little brighter.

"You two get back in here *this instant*!" shouts a nurse behind us.

After a long lecture and some very skilled apologizing on Henry's part, a very pissed off nurse escorts us back to my room.

"We'll find a way," he says as soon as we are alone.

"Where would we even go?" I ask.

"We could stay at that hotel in the Loop and go catch a movie before the jig is up."

"Henry, listen, we can't."

He stops and that glimmer of frustration crosses his forehead.

"It'll be okay," he says. "I promise. I'll say I made you do it. If you can't stay, then I want to take you home."

He kneels in front of the wheelchair, his arms resting on my lap.

"Let me do the thinking for the both of us this time, kid. I will take care of you," he says. "Always."

"But that's the problem. If we do this, it's forever," I say.

"No," he says, laughing. "Though it's probably the rest of the summer grounded for you and probably no more car for either of us."

He smiles. I love his smile.

"But, Sadie . . . I do want forever. I want forever with you."

I can see the crossroads beneath us, one path leaving with Henry, one path back to the hospital room. But it seems, either way, the destination is the same. Not a crossroads, but a highway with different lanes. There are forks in the road for some people, but for me, it's always been a highway that doesn't go anywhere but the horizon, never-ending.

My road always ends with Henry. I can never decide if that's good or bad.

"Let's do it right. I'll stay," I say. "I don't want you to get in trouble."

Relief washes over his face.

"It's only a few more days," Henry says as he helps me up into the bed. "And I will come back for every one of them if you want."

"No," I say. "I don't want to be a bother."

"You're not a bother," he snaps. He pulls away. "Why would I be coming here if you were a bother?"

"You think I'm more special than I am."

"Darling, don't talk like that," Henry says. I hate it when he quotes things at me. He tries too hard. He gets it from movies, and sometimes I can even see the scene he's imitating in my head because we saw it together. And it seems so wrong when those words come out of his mouth, because he's not Paul Henreid, he's Henry, and I *want* him to be Henry and it's like he doesn't know that.

"But you do," I insist. "I'm dragging you down."

He grits his teeth.

I see it, like a predator in the bush: his secrets. All the things he wants to say and ask. All the things he holds back. The fight we've been waiting to have is lurking behind his lips. I watch him let it loose.

"Well, okay. Maybe I do think you're special. But you think I'm more special than I am too. You remember me being awesome at guitar this whole time. And like, yeah, I was pretty good . . . for a ninth grader. You remember me being cool when we met. I've never felt cool. Even now, who do you think thinks I'm so 'cool'? You think you felt like a loser spending your days alone in the summer before

185

we started hanging out. Who was there with you? I was there every day too. Alone. People think I'm a suck-up because my mom is a teacher. That I'm a weirdo who only thinks about guitars. Or people don't think about me at all.

"You do this to Lucie too. You worship her, put her on a pedestal. But you and Lucie are totally the same: you like the same nerdy stuff, you run together, you hang out at school, laugh at the same stuff . . . so why do you pretend that you're her sidekick? You know she thinks she's *your* sidekick, right? I don't understand girls. *No one is the sidekick.*

"So yeah, I think you're special, and I think you're smart. And I wish . . . you didn't always have to make that into a challenge. Can't you just be happy that I like you? And you like me? You don't always think about other people. Their feelings. You think you do, because you *see* a lot about people. But sometimes I think it's all about you."

"That's a really jerky thing to say," I snap.

"Yeah? Well, it's true. You know . . . ugh . . . what is that movie you like? *Now, Voyager*? With the self-pitying, self-obsessed lady?"

"Yeah?" This is very dangerous territory. Also, one hundred percent not how I would describe that movie.

"I know why you love that movie. It's because you're *just like her.*"

Now, Voyager is my favorite movie of all time. We saw it just before Henry went away. It's a love story. In the movie, Charlotte Vale (played by Bette Davis) is an old maid and a crazy person, but she falls in love with a man named Jerry, who is played by the ultracool Paul Henreid, who loves her right back from the moment he sees her for who she really is: someone who feels like she is only pretending to be special. In the movie he does this thing where he lights two cigarettes and gives her one. Paul Henreid couldn't go anywhere in the world without women asking him to light cigarettes for them, according to Wikipedia.

I *love* this movie. I love everything about it, but maybe what I love best is the last scene.

Spoiler alert: Charlotte and Jerry don't end up together. They have to forfeit their love so that they can fulfill their obligations in life. That's just fate. And so Jerry says, "Shall we just have a cigarette on it?" and he lights two cigarettes, and he gives one to Charlotte. And then right at the end he asks her, "Will you be happy, Charlotte?" And Charlotte says, "Oh, Jerry, don't let's ask for the moon. We have the stars."

And then there's this perfect, poetic closing shot that goes up, up, and shows the night sky with only the stars and it is so beautiful. I love that part. And that's the end.

"I am not just like her. First of all, she's an old maid," I say, but then I can't come up with a lot of other reasons. So instead I snap: "What's wrong with her, anyway?"

"She's a brat!" Henry shouts. He glances at the door. The nurses are going to come in here. We quiet down.

"You don't understand what it's like to feel bad about yourself," I say, trying to stay quiet.

"There you go again."

"I feel like I'm no one," I tell him weakly. "But it's not that simple. I can't explain it. I feel like . . . like . . ."

"Like what? Why can't you just tell me something *real,* for once? Something *true?*"

He sits down in the chair in my room so we are looking eye to eye, but he stands up again quickly. He reaches under the seat and pulls out a red notebook. My heart thumps.

"Is this yours?" he asks.

"No, I think someone left it in here," I say. I snatch it from him and put it on the nightstand. Eleanor has saved me from myself yet again. *How did that get in here?* I wonder.

"You were saying?" Henry asks. But I don't feel like explaining it anymore. I'm not even sure if I could make him understand, because I don't quite understand myself.

"Nothing."

He comes over and puts his hand on my face and looks directly into my eyes the way I hate, so intense it's like he is trying to take something from me.

"Someday, you are going to tell me the truth. Someday I'm going to find out what is behind your eyes. But I'll tell you my half of our truth now."

I want to stop him, but I can't even speak. I'm hypnotized.

"I don't care if you don't believe me. I think you're special," Henry says. "You're not holding me back. You know what you give me? You make me feel like someone sees the real me and likes me anyway. And you make me feel important. You have these whole worlds in your head full of all the weird things you like. And the fact that you think I'm as interesting as all those things makes me feel like a hero. Like I'm interesting.

"And I love our curiosity, and our habits, and our silliness, and our inside jokes. I love that I can rely on you, and that you want so badly not to hurt me that you are willing to totally ruin our relationship just so you won't hurt my feelings. I love that you care that much.

"And you know what? I think you're so beautiful. I mean, so sexy. Like, you drive me crazy. I can't say it as well as you can, and I don't know what the right word is, but whatever perfect movie quote you have up your sleeve, can you please pretend I said that? Because you'll never understand how much I want you unless I can say it in your language, and I don't speak it yet. I'm still trying to learn.

"You have such beautiful eyes. I will always think you are the most perfect person in the world. I will *never* love anyone this much. I want us to be together forever."

"Henry . . ." I try to think of what to say, trying to stop him from saying anything more. That's the worst thing: Henry's secrets aren't anything more than the truth, *our* truth, that he holds on to for us both. It's too much. I can't hear it. But I can't say anything because I'm so happy and so sad and so everything.

I know that I love him. I know that he meant what he said. He's always been that way: certain.

But I'm not. I don't deserve him.

We talk and we touch and we kiss the way that we always do, and it all flies by in that happy light he carries with him, burning everything else away. He leaves and I expect the darkness to come flooding back. But it doesn't, for minutes, then hours, and I'm somehow still glowing. I'm left with only the truth of us:

Henry is my still harbor, my anchor, even when I'm out to sea.

I don't want him, because I don't believe in forever.

But then he's here, and I do.

WILL AND WON'T

Sadie and Henry were breathless, hands clasped as they cuddled across the gap between the seats, eyes on the screen. Up there in shades of gray, framed by red curtains, Paul Henreid and Bette Davis were falling in love as they did every time the movie played. For them, every time, it was brand-new. For Sadie and Henry it felt new too.

As Sadie watched the closing scene, she felt her stomach turn. Even sitting in the movie theater curled under Henry's heavy arm, Sadie couldn't help but see George in black-and-white on the screen. He was always with her. She hated herself for thinking of George every time she remembered whose hand she was holding, whose Old Spice smell she was breathing amid the fake butter.

They left the Tivoli Theatre—their special spot—in a strange mood. Sadie was distracted. Henry didn't even ask her where she was in her head. He'd stopped trying.

Sadie tried to gather herself, to be there for Henry. She had to. As Henry threw away the popcorn, she shook her head as hard as she could, jumbling brain cells, clearing her mind. When he came back, she had her smiling mask on.

"Race you?" she asked. He laughed. He could see she was back.

They were addicted to the Tivoli. Leaving the theater they were always strangely electric, whether from the story on the screen or sitting skin to skin in the dark. They sprinted to the car. She reveled in the stolen minutes in Henry's backseat. That true, real romance took her spiraling into the present.

But she was so afraid even then, even while kissing him. There was always that voice in the back of her head, observing and shaming her. But he didn't know. He couldn't possibly know what shameful things she had thought in the dark of the theater, her shameful love of someone who wasn't and never would be real, and her constant shameful need for that other world.

Henry's mouth. Henry's eyes. Henry's hands. She focused on those things.

When they were together, talking and laughing and touching, she felt real, sometimes just for a moment. But she couldn't stay.

She was never free. The pull of other worlds caught her heels wherever she went.

*

When Henry dropped her off after seeing *Now, Voyager*, they gave each other a chaste kiss in case anyone was watching, and Sadie ran inside. She didn't know why she was so shy about it. After all, Henry was graduating in a month, and next year she'd be a senior. They'd been dating forever. They were unendingly seeking closed doors behind which to commit carnal acts, and the game of secrets brought them closer. They'd found a lot of closed doors that year. But she always felt like if anyone saw them together in public, their love affair would evaporate: like having Henry was imaginary somehow.

Everything felt imaginary, more and more.

She muttered a greeting to her parents. She didn't even take off her shoes. She went straight downstairs, to her room.

Another world was calling. She could barely keep herself from falling out of this one.

On her desktop computer, she paged through link after link, absorbing every detail of *Now, Voyager*. The production. Interviews with the cast. She consumed it all. She'd seen this one before, she was certain, but she couldn't remember it at all. It had been hiding in a locked box, which she had inadvertently opened with a movie ticket.

"The untold want by life and land ne'er granted / Now, voyager, sail thou forth to seek and find." The poem echoed in her mind. Whitman. She'd known those words, but now they exploded with meaning, every word a firework. But what did it *really* mean? The Internet had so many opinions on that.

To seek and find. It was such a tiny phrase, but now she felt it meant so much. Wasn't that what she was meant to do?

Her mind went out, seeking fantasies.

She paused, looking at the clock. Two a.m. She'd been online for hours, lulled senseless by gentle waves of browsing. For the past few months she'd been falling into the Internet. She would spend hours awash in pictures and articles. Her desktop was a collage of links and files and ideas. All her school binders were filled with facts she had no use for. She'd barely done her homework in weeks.

How had she gotten to two in the morning? Time vanished. She had school the next day.

As soon as she wasn't with Henry, she felt like she didn't even exist. Not in the real world. Everything felt like a daydream.

And the worst of it was, even though she felt bad, and even though she wanted to want only Henry, she desperately missed George.

At home, the shame was worse and worse. It beat at her consciousness, dragging her out like the tide. She tried to stay busy. She tried to keep her mind on Henry, on the real. But tonight, something about the movie had tripped her. It had been too perfect. A subtly shifting figure lit two cigarettes and mused about happiness. Sometimes it was Paul

Henreid. Sometimes Henry. Sometimes George. Sometimes it seemed to be all three.

The undertow had pulled her down. She was already out to sea. The rush of the tide became whispers and—

No. She shook her head as hard as she could until her ears rang and her mind was blank. She looked at the floor of her messy room, ignoring all the books and adventures, ignoring temptation. But everything was temptation.

If she tried to sleep, she would lie half-awake, half-dreaming for hours. She grabbed her backpack from under her bed and dug around for overdue assignments. School was never hard, so she would never fail, but sliding by made her stomach turn. She used to like being homeschooled. She even liked real school sometimes. But she didn't like anything anymore, really. Even obsessing over movies didn't feel like liking something.

She focused on her AP physics homework and the concepts of distance and time and speed and what they all meant, and how she could never go back and relive the time she had lost to dreaming or get back the things she had missed. She remembered the cruelty of what Einstein had said about time: "The distinction between the past, present, and future is only a stubbornly persistent illusion." So forever, she would be locked in this cycle of regret. She would have given anything to vanish out of time.

"Come away with me," George whispered behind her, his lips on the back of her ear.

The world was already narrowing and falling away. Once more, she was gone.

*

The ballroom fell to a hush as Sadie entered. It was full of static and strangers, eyes glittering in the candlelight like those of predators.

Sadie's white dress swept the floor as she made her way into the unfamiliar room. Her jacket was embroidered with a butterfly, and she would have given anything to escape on those borrowed wings. Her heart raced in time to the orchestra.

"Miss," a familiar voice called behind her. She turned too quickly, her nose suddenly facing a gold button.

"George, I thought we were being discreet."

"This is discreet. It's perfectly discreet to dance with a lovely unexpected guest."

"Not in this dress, it's not. Where did you find this?"

"Well, I had to dispose of the femme fatale who wore it last, but it seemed a shame to let it go to waste."

"We can't be seen together."

"Indulge me," he said, taking her hand.

"I can't."

"Of course you can. The question is, do you want to?"

"Unequivocally."

"Then just follow me."

"I always try."

He let her have the last word, leading her to the floor. The murmurs of the crowd resumed and they were invisible once again. They fell into the familiar rhythm: one two three, one two three. But as they twirled, George winced.

"You're hurt," Sadie whispered, peeking under his jacket. Blood bloomed over his heart.

"Shot, I'm afraid."

"George!"

"I wanted to say goodbye in case I don't make it. One should always say a proper goodbye—it's the most important part of dying."

"I can help you!"

"No, it's too dangerous."

"You dress me up like a spy, teach me to think like one, but now that there's something real to do, it's over?"

"Not for you. It's just beginning for you. But I'm racing time, Sadie. My number is up."

"What do you mean?"

"They know my face. I've been made, darling."

Sadie glanced over George's shoulder. She could see men in black suits with dark eyes scanning the crowd. George kissed her lightly on the cheek and pulled away, but Sadie clung to him.

"I only want what's best for you," George said. "You've got to let me go."

"Let me come with you." The music slowed and they stopped in the middle of the floor.

"Darling, I would never want to take you where I must go. I'm dying, love. I'm made. I'm already dead."

"Why do you have to go? Can't we run away together? Can't we escape?"

"Sadie," he started, breaking character. He looked at her as himself, as her best friend, and continued: "Sadie, you can't run forever. This isn't escaping. We never really get away. We're just going in circles. Can't you feel it? Something is wrong." Her heart broke open as she felt herself slipping; she was not a spy, she was only Sadie, and she didn't want to hear. There were other memories seeping into this one. The stars above looked like shards of glass. He opened his mouth to say more, but she kissed him before he could. Time stopped.

And then he pulled away, and they were both spies again, and the real world was forgotten.

Everyone was staring. The men in black suits threaded the crowd.

"Stay," she pleaded. His escape was cut off. His eyes read the room and decided on the regrettable: a shootout. "Please, George. We'll do this together. Take me with you."

He didn't like to be challenged, but he too had a streak of selfishness in love. He was dangerous, beautiful, and angry, and he was going to say yes. She watched his face soften as he came to the same realization. What bliss it was to anticipate. She put her hand on her gun, ready to go down fighting rather than be taken prisoner. There were so few surprises for a spy as clever as she. But the inevitable was no less intoxicating in these rapidly escalating moments—

✳

They were back in Sadie's basement.

"What happened?" Sadie gasped.

"I'm done," George said.

It was as though an episode had been cut short by an emergency broadcast. Sadie could feel the cliff-hanger in the air. Something had changed.

"What do you mean you're done?"

"I mean I'm done with this. All of this."

Sadie's voice crumbled. "With me?"

"With all of this! With the wish fulfillment and the romance and the bullshit! And these games! How does it always end up the same?"

"We're just . . . having fun." She wanted to put her arms around him, but she was afraid.

"Fun? You think this is *fun*?"

"If you don't like me anymore . . ."

"Like you? *Like* you? What is there to like? Who are you, Sadie? Who are you without me?"

Her heart was racing.

"Who am I? Who are you?"

"I'm whatever you want me to be!" George shouted. "God damn it!"

He knocked everything off her desk, worlds clattering

to the floor. One hand flew to his brow, and from between long fingers he glared at her. Then he marched right up to her. She could feel his breath.

"And oh, what glory, being a girl's fantasy. Princes and poetry. Spies. Great romances. Tragic romances. But nothing real. You're afraid of anything messy. If it isn't movie magic, it isn't good enough for you. But that's not real, and you know it! There's nothing real about love anymore. . . ." He trailed off, shaking his head, grinning like the devil. "Oh, Sadie, with *you* it'll never be anything more than an act. You don't love me. You don't know what love is.

"And do you think that's fair to me? Making me this demented Prince Charming you've imagined all for yourself? Is that who you think I want to be? Constantly clever, constantly perfect. Never sweats, never shits, never has a moment of weakness or an unkind thought. It isn't fair.

"You don't care about me. You only care about what satisfies your childish dreams. You want a story, not a flawed, living person. You only want what fits into your fantasy. You're getting a little old for that, Sadie. And I'm getting tired of treating you like a child."

"Then leave," Sadie snarled.

"I can't! Do you think I want this?" George gasped, so angry he didn't have the breath left to yell. "Do you think that I want to be stuck here, with *you* for eternity, all because you thought of me? Do you think I want what has been set out for me?"

"George . . ."

"You think you're special. You think you're this tragic hero. It's all you've ever wanted: to be fascinating, to be interesting. But you're not. Not without me. Well, I'm sorry you've damned yourself to this boring nothing of a life, but I don't want this. I don't want to be trapped here."

"You're not trapped in anything! You're not real!"

Crack!

The shock of the slap made her ears ring. She felt the hardness of him, the bones in the back of his hand as it threw her off her feet, the hot metal of his ring.

"Don't you ever say that," George said, kneeling close to her on the floor, his finger pointed straight at her heart. "Don't you ever, *ever* say that."

Sadie was quiet, biting back tears. George leaned forward and kissed her and then vanished.

DAY 9

Henry. Henry. Henry.

I basked in the afterglow of Henry all yesterday, even after he left. It got me all the way through Day 8 of my confinement, and I slept right through the night.

I smile as I write his name over and over. I like the shape of the letters, the straight lines of the *H*'s. But even as dawn breaks on Day 9, that warm thrill of Henry gets sanitized by the too-bright lights and the medicinal soap and the breakfast I don't want. The hospital closes in and he's no more than yesterday's memory and I'm alone. And sitting all alone with no one but myself to judge me, I have in my hands a document that a better person would not open. I struggle valiantly with the morality of what I know I am about to do. But if you end up doing the wrong thing, then you were going to do the wrong thing all along, right? All those near misses of doing the right thing, they don't count even a little bit, because of how the story ends. The idea that you might count them, and that the chances were a million to one . . . that's a fallacy, if you believe in destiny. If you believe in destiny, then the chances were always one hundred percent that you would do the wrong thing.

I run my hand over the cover of Eleanor's red journal, the twin of my own.

I never could resist an unread book.

You know when you read the back cover of a book and you get so into it, because the idea of the story is so awesome? And even before you've read it, you're super-excited just to get to spend time in that world with those people? That's about how well I know Eleanor. She is a book jacket: all promise.

But I already feel like I know her so well! She's that kind of story: the kind that you know was written just for you. I love the idea of Eleanor and her boyfriend sneaking around Paris on boarding school holidays, smoking in alleyways. When I picture them, a whole world springs out of an image: they wear black leather jackets, and her hair is newly dyed in that rainbow of pastels. He doesn't speak much English, so they both speak French, and when he holds her the spikes on his jacket press into her skin, but she doesn't mind. I can suffer the joyful sharpness of how it would feel to be held by someone bad like that.

I want to read that life.

I flip open the cover with my eyes closed, and I think hard about not opening them because I know what I'm doing is wrong.

But I open them.

I read a few pages and my stomach turns.

I should have remembered: a book with an awesome premise doesn't always live up to its cover.

It couldn't be, I think to myself. This is wrong. So I take out the note Eleanor left me. I flip toward the back, and hold its rough edges to a torn page I find there: a perfect jigsaw fit. I compare the handwriting. I use every trick of reasonable disbelief to try to dismantle the truth, but it's too late: I know, and I can't unknow.

The notebook is definitely hers.

Little phrases jump out at me:

No one loves me. I hate school. I would give anything to go to boarding school.

I am nothing. No one. I am invisible.

If I died, maybe I would wake up as someone else.

I can't feel anything until I hurt myself, and even then I feel nothing.

I read sentence after sentence and everything I know about her falls away until all that is left is Eleanor, who is just like me: a big melodramatic liar, trying to make something important that isn't.

I pull my green notebook out and open it on top of Eleanor's. But I'm at a loss for words.

"Day 9," I write:

I just want to go home.

✳

I think I'm ready. Henry still loves me. He doesn't know about George. No one does. As long as no one finds out, everything can go back to how it used to be. Even at my most vulnerable, I kept George safe.

I am unsinkable.

But nothing is unsinkable, I remind myself. That thought passing through my brain and onto paper feels like an omen.

Even so, I'm actually excited when the nurses wheel me into Dr. Roberts's office. I even do some of the wheeling myself. But before I can say anything, she puts one finger up.

"I have to ask you a question that might be a little uncomfortable," she says. "I don't want you to feel ambushed, but you must remember, there is a reason you are here. And I would be remiss to simply allow you to continue talking around it. Now, I've spoken to your parents—"

"You did *what*!"

"And I asked them if they happened to know of any of your friends who might be named George. And do you know what they told me? I have a feeling you do."

And I swear, I can feel my heart stop.

✳

I say nothing.

I didn't see it coming. You never do, these big things. You remember them, and later it seems like they were inevitable. But that's just ordering the past into an arrow to the present. Memory makes stories out of time. You naturally destroy the things that you forgot along the way. All the red herrings and alternate worlds don't live on in memory. They're lost as the arrow of your story shoots by.

I am always asking after those lost things. Where are the events that are not in the past, present, or future? What happens to all those forgotten thoughts? If no one remembers something, did it even really happen?

I don't want to remember this.

The world is backing out of my consciousness and pulling away down that long tunnel, like a train leaving me behind. The office where we sit becomes a collection of objects: a pen, a chair, a nail, a desk, a book, a book, a book . . . I look at my hands. They seem a million miles away.

I can see George, in the phantom way dreams happen. He's not really there. What would he say? *Keep your mouth shut. Don't you dare answer. Do you want me to die?* No, that isn't it. He'd know it was only an accident. He would know I couldn't stop it.

But even if it was an accident, it can still be my fault.

"Sadie?" Roberts calls. When I don't respond, she says, "I know you don't want to talk about this. Can you answer me?"

I stare at the books over her shoulder and start counting them, since each one I count lifts me higher and farther away. The universe is chaotic, but numbers are peaceful. They arrange themselves neatly in lines and squares, in ways that make sense, in ways that can be understood. I love counting. One. Two. Three . . . *Eleven . . . One thousand . . .*

George, smiling at Sadie from across the room.

His hands in Sadie's hair, whispering, "Quiet, darling. Everything will be all right. I'm here. I'm always here."

Sadie cried in her mind, but her face wasn't connected to her thoughts anymore. She didn't have a body, it seemed. She was at once scared and happy. She didn't understand how it had happened, but her wish came true.

Sadie was with George.

"Sadie. Let's just sit here for a moment," Dr. Roberts said, far away. "I'm going to sit here and when you're ready, you can say whatever you want to say, and then we'll go on or we'll stop. It's up to you. I think you can hear me. Sadie."

Sadie . . .

Where is she?

THE RIDDLE HOUSE

Sadie had both hands on the ears of the German shepherd. She felt like a little kid, even though she was almost seventeen. For kids, everything is new and alien and wonderful. Petting a dog could be an adventure if you were little enough. This dog had ears that made her feel like that, and for just a moment the gray fog that smothered every day lifted.

She really wasn't sure if that was how you were supposed to pet his ears—she'd never had a dog—but she couldn't stop playing with them. They were huge. The dog's face was old, graying. His name was Sirius, and he was not particularly enthusiastic about the prospect of running. He kept lying down whenever she tried to warm him up. He seemed like the kind of dog who would prefer to sleep, and Sadie liked that.

"What's up, cocaptain? I got this little wiener," Lucie said, walking up next to her with a long squirming sausage of a mutt in her arms. "She's a wiener, but I can tell she's a winner."

"My dog's name is Sirius." Sadie showed her the tag.

"You should ask your parents if you can take him home," Lucie said. "I want this one, but we already have too many fosters."

Lucie wandered away, cooing at the dog as though she'd never seen one before. "We'll find you a place to belong," Lucie sang.

It was the start of summer before her senior year. Sadie was sure it was too late to get a dog. How would she take it with her into a dorm room? Sadie looked into Sirius's big, dark eyes. They were trusting and understanding. When she walked away, he followed. He seemed like a loyal companion.

"Or a sidekick," George said, petting Sirius. Sirius grinned amiably, rolling over. George seemed to like him too.

When she had started cross-country right before high school, Sadie had loved running for the time with George: practices were long, boring stretches of green she could hazily dream through. But Lucie wouldn't let her dream. They stayed in step, in the present, side by side, captain and vice captain. It had been easy to get lost in Lucie instead of George until they both reached that silent, crystal-clear plane of endorphin high. But something without a name had changed, moving in and colonizing her, and she was slipping back into dreams. It was getting harder and harder. . . . Lucie talked and Sadie could barely hear her with George siphoning off her attention.

"All right, warriors!" shouted Lucie, and the whole team perked up. "Stay on the sidewalks, look after your dog, and don't run too hard. Let's have some fun!"

All around her, pit bulls and labs and Chihuahuas and girls trotted off into the leafy neighborhood. Lucie, who was normally in the lead, had already started to lag behind. She was shouting, "Come on, Snickers!" and jogging backward, trying to coax the short-legged dog forward.

Sadie tugged on Sirius's leash and started jogging. He loped along like an old man. But after a few steps, it was like he remembered better days. He ran hard, in step with her.

They left the rest of the girls behind. Sadie and Sirius were running without thinking, completely in tune.

"Don't stop," George panted next to her. Sirius was looking around, scouting for danger with his unrivaled sense of smell. The cobblestones beneath their feet were difficult to navigate, but the three of them flew down the road. George glanced at his watch. "We've got fifteen minutes to make the drop."

Sirius, vigilant even in a sprint, barked as he smelled an enemy. George pulled out his revolver—

"Sadie, watch out!"

She'd run straight into the street, and right in front of a car. Startled, she dropped Sirius's leash. The car leaned on its horn, the driver shouting. Terrified, Sirius darted away, narrowly missing an oncoming car. He charged down the street, faster than Sadie had ever seen a dog run.

Sadie sprinted after him, but he was going too fast. She'd never catch him.

"Cut him off!" shouted Lucie behind her.

Sadie's mind turned off, and she was all legs, all speed. She veered off the road and into a series of luxurious backyards, crashing through flowers and swing sets and tiny decorative fences. She could hear the horns in the road as the few cars driving in the neighborhood watched a German shepherd racing down the street. Thank God it wasn't crowded.

She emerged back on the road. Sadie could see Lucie in the corner of her eye, running just as hard. Lucie was running wide. They'd had the same idea: Lucie was going to follow up from behind in case Sadie scared him backward.

She'd managed to get just ahead of him. "Sirius!" She shouted with what little breath she had. She jumped to grab him by the collar, but she felt his fur slip through her fingers instead. She landed with a hard crash on the asphalt, scraping her knees bloody. Lucie was feet behind her. At the last moment, Sadie grabbed Sirius's leash and with a hard yank, brought him tumbling down. He let out a pitiful yelp as his collar choked him.

She crawled toward the whimpering dog. He cowered from her.

"What were you thinking?" Lucie screamed.

"It was an accident," Sadie said, trying to calm Sirius, who was panting hard. He cried and cried. Sadie petted him. She knew exactly how he felt: a brush with death that shuts down your entire mind, even though your body is fine. She knew what it was like to feel real fear.

"You *weren't* thinking. You were being a goddamn absentminded idiot, like you always are. What if a car had hit him! What if it had hit *you*?"

Sadie grabbed the leash firmly and stood up. Sirius pulled away but wasn't strong enough to run again.

"It was an accident," she said again, struggling with the dog.

"Are you stupid? You can *cause* an accident, Sadie! Just because it was an accident doesn't mean no one is to blame!" Lucie shouted.

And then Sadie burst into tears.

*

The dogs had been taken back to the shelter and all the other girls had gone home, but Sadie sat alone on the curb waiting for her parents to pick her up. The sky grew dark and the wind howled. Sadie shivered. She let her mind wander, but she was too angry to think of George. She thought of telling her parents she would never run again. The pleasure of arguing in her head passed the time, but even that grew dim. After half an hour, she stood and started pacing. It was getting cold. After an hour, she pulled out her phone and texted her dad, but he didn't answer. She called her mom, but no one picked up.

Lucie had apologized, and so had Sadie. But she was still angry at herself, and sad for Sirius. She would have liked to take him home, but she didn't deserve him. She deserved to be alone.

The wind rustled the leaves above. She sat on the curb, curled up her knees, and counted the seconds as they ticked by.

She barely noticed when Old Charlotte rolled to a squealing stop in front of her.

Her mother swung open the driver's-side door. The windows were still wrecked and inoperable. Her dad waved from the passenger's seat.

"Did you have fun?" he called.

"You're late," Sadie said. She could feel her face getting red, tears of mysterious origin piling up in her eyes. She shook them away. There was no reason to be upset.

"Sorry, sweetie. Last-minute customers. Maybe it's time to try for your license again."

"It's fine," Sadie said curtly. She was squished between her parents. She was way too big to be sitting in the middle. Her mom nearly killed it trying to get the car in gear.

"So . . . we didn't have fun," her dad said.

"Brilliant observation."

"Hey," her mom said sharply.

They rode in silence for several minutes, save the screech of Old Charlotte's brakes.

"Why didn't you go out with the other girls tonight?"

"I just want to go home. Henry has band practice."

"What about Lucie?"

"She's got better things to do. She just got a puppy."

The car was full of silence for too long. They pulled up to a stoplight and they were left only with the rumble of Old Charlotte.

"Maybe . . . you could try and make some more friends?" her dad suggested.

"I have friends."

"You have Henry and Lucie," her mom said. Her dad shifted uncomfortably. "And God knows we love them, but don't you think you might want more friends? You spend all day in the basement on that computer."

"I'm doing schoolwork," Sadie said.

"Sure," her mom said.

"I like being alone. I'm used to it," Sadie said.

"What does that mean?"

Sadie said nothing. As long as no one said anything, everything would always be all right. *What is nothing plus nothing?* she wondered.

"Whatever," Sadie mumbled, her heart pounding. She was angry and she didn't know why. Who did she have to be angry with but herself? She swallowed her rage, focused on her breathing. Deep, rageful breaths so hard they made her hands shake. She reached out to the radio.

"Don't turn it on. We'll never get it off."

Sadie crossed her arms; then, with a compulsion she

would later be unable to explain, she reached out and turned the radio on anyway.

"Sadie, you know this thing only plays static." Her dad pushed the buttons in random patterns, trying to convince it to give up its half-hearted attempt to find the music lost in the noise.

"Here, let me do it," her mom said, one hand on the wheel, one fiddling with the radio.

"Stop! Watch what you're doing!" Sadie yelled. The sound of overwhelmingly loud static filled the car, like psychological torture. Somehow the radio switched to the tape player, and they recoiled as the tail end of "Here Comes the Sun" began playing.

Sadie's heart sank. Her mom's foot stepped off the gas as she recognized The Tape. Sadie watched the color drain from her father's face as he first doubted, and then wondered how The Tape could have possibly gotten into this car to be deployed at this moment.

The music continued. They didn't speak for the rest of the way home. Sadie could feel her heart hitting her rib cage, and wondered what her parents felt.

They pulled into the driveway and sat for a moment.

"Can we just go inside?"

"How long has that tape been in here?" her dad asked over the music.

Her mom said: "It must have been playing when we—"

"Yes, but this is the radio I put in right when we started restoring her years ago—"

The song got louder so she had to yell over The Tape.

"*I put it in there and it got stuck!*" Sadie yelled. "Now can we *please* go inside?"

Her parents didn't move. She often wondered if they really remembered the crash. They'd been so torn up, she doubted it.

Her mom turned off the car and the music stopped.

"I don't remember it, but that must have been what was playing when we crashed," her mom said, looking at them both. "Do you remember? It sends a chill right through you."

"I don't remember either," said her dad.

"Me neither. Now can we please get out of the car?" Sadie snapped. Her parents obliged slowly, as they always were these days.

"Aren't you coming in?" her mom asked. Sadie was still standing in the driveway.

"No," Sadie said. Her parents didn't ask her any questions. They went inside, lost in memories. She watched as the lights turned on in their offices on the second floor. Through those windows, her parents were like pictures in frames.

Things were so much simpler now. How was it that every day was also so much harder? It was like a riddle without an answer. Sometimes a riddle is just a meaningless string of words. She looked up at the lights in the house.

She felt like a picture on a wall staring across at other pictures, pretending to see them with painted eyes. Every person in the whole world was a lonely piece of beautiful art.

That's all people are, she thought as she looked at the windows above. *We're just frames gazing at frames.*

✳

"Hello, darling," George said, his shoes crunching on the gravel. He crouched next to her and wrote his name in the loose rocks while she cried until she was dry-heaving. Every sob shook her whole body.

"Are you done yet?" He looked up at her.

Sadie couldn't speak. She was still as stone, like a miracle statue doomed to weep blood as evidence of a higher power. And all the people would come to see her cry and say, "It's proof of God," but no one would ever ask how it felt to cry for eternity.

George reached up and wrapped his fingers around her clenched fist. His hands were so much larger than hers.

"You know I'd bring you a star if you'd let me. But we have to get out of the driveway," George said softly. He stood and put his arm around her. They walked into the backyard to the old bench swing. The waterproof pads were wet and slick, and when she sat down the whole contraption screamed.

"What's wrong?" George asked, as though he didn't know.

"I'm all alone," Sadie choked out. George sat in the

grass with a weary thump. Sadie lay sideways on the swing, hypnotized by his eyes. He pushed the swing, drawing her closer and farther away, to and from him.

"Darling. Don't cry," George said. "Come on, Sadie. Where's somewhere you've always wanted to go?"

He stopped the swing and put his hand over her eyes.

"We can go anywhere. We can do anything. Just you and me. Let's go."

She kept her eyes closed, and the whole world disappeared. The whole world, except for George and the constellations above.

DAY 12

I'm not awake. Not really. I'm somewhere else. But I can feel myself being drawn back. Down the hall, I hear them calling: *Eleanor.* As people pass by my open door, I hear her name standing out from the muffled static.

I open my eyes, and for the first time in a few days, I feel like I'm seeing through them. It's strange to be back.

It's happened before. The world passes over me like I'm underwater, looking up from the bottom of the ocean.

I want to see Eleanor so badly that I rise to the surface again. I feel George's fingers slipping out of mine, and I promise I will return. I leave that safe half-state of dreams, back into the ache of existence.

I wheel myself down to Eleanor's room before anyone thinks to interrogate me about my return to wakefulness. She's sitting up in bed, but right away I can see that something isn't right.

She's tied up in a hospital gown, her shark costume nowhere in sight. Her hair is falling out. When she looks at me, she turns her head slowly, pivoting with an almost audible ache.

"Eleanor?" I ask, but she doesn't look up.

"Eleanor, it's Sadie," I try again. "Remember me?"

"No, I don't remember you. I'm sorry." She speaks so quietly I almost don't hear her.

She lies down facing me, watching me with disinterest like a screen saver.

"What happened to you?" I ask. "Where did they take you?"

"ECT," she says.

"What?"

"Electro . . . something."

"Like . . . shock therapy?" I shriek. Is she telling me the truth? It would be like her to lie. She looks bemused at my horror, and for a moment I see her rise from wherever she's hiding in her mind.

"I know you," Eleanor says. "I *do* sort of remember you. How long have you been here?"

"Almost two weeks," I tell her.

"It's usually the recent things that vanish, so that explains it. ECT sounds worse than it is, so don't freak out if that's what you're here for."

"It's not."

"It's not usually what I do either. But nothing else works. It can help."

I feel like I'm choking.

"You're not Eleanor," I say.

"Of course I am. Look at the door. Mary Eleanor Smith."

"No, you told me they'd change you." Tears well up in my eyes.

She leans toward me, teeth bared. "*I* am *me*. This is who I really am. That other person . . . she's crazy. She's ruining my life. I hate her. The girl you know? That Eleanor? I hate her."

"But you . . . are her," I say.

"Sometimes it feels like I'm two people. I'm me. And then I'm the version of me I hate, who does these things that I hate. It hurts so much to remember what I do and not understand how it's possible that someone could behave that way. How is it possible to feel so out of control? I have to believe that I am someone else when I get that way. And I'm so happy to kill her, you know? I want her to die."

She looks at her arms mournfully.

"Maybe that's how I keep ending up this way," she says. "If I have to be both, I'd rather be neither."

"What are you saying?" I ask. Her eyes fill with tears.

"If you can get well," she says, her voice breaking. "If you can get well and get out of here, do it. Listen to this version of me."

She takes a deep and crackling breath, wiping her eyes.

"You told me he hurts you," she says. "I remember now. Your boyfriend hurts you."

"No, that wasn't it. George doesn't hurt me. He can't," I say, racing to cut off the spiral of her thoughts. "He loves me, remember?"

"Oh. I remember," she says, leaning back into her pillow. She seems relieved. Then that strange look comes over her eyes, like a glimmer of the old Eleanor.

"I met a boy named George here once," Eleanor says.

"What did he say?" I whisper.

"He was so scared. He said all of this isn't real. He said they've got it backward . . . that they're killing him."

She closes her eyes. "He must have been crazy. I don't even know if he was real."

"What is real, anyway?" I say under my breath. She glares at me.

"He *isn't* real, your George. Is he?" she says.

"No," I reply. She sits up and looks at me very seriously.

"Then you need to get rid of him. You have to leave him behind." She says it with the cruel detachment of some adult who has told her the same thing.

"Eleanor, what are you saying?"

"I'm saying exactly what you need to hear. Listen, he's not your friend. I know exactly what he is: he's a sickness. He's not real. You need to leave him."

"How can you say that? How could I ever leave him?" I squeak, my throat closing with tears. "I thought you understood."

"I do understand."

"No you don't. *Eleanor* did. So what, he's not real. I know that. I've *always* known that. But what is so great about real? So what, I have George. So I'd rather be with George. Why wouldn't I want that when my life is the endless ticking of a clock of suck that will never go anywhere and nothing will ever get better? Why would I want to live in this world when I can be with him?

"We have fallen in love a hundred million times. He is my best friend. He has died in my arms, and I have died in his. And he will never leave. So how could I ever leave him? He's not my soul mate. He's me."

She just looks at me with pity, and the pity makes me hate her.

I want to hurt her.

I want to do something cruel.

"I know you understand," I say. I take out her journal and hold it out to her. I can see her putting the pieces together, her face growing darker.

"I found it in my room."

"It's not mine," she says. I put it on the bed next to her. She picks it up and throws it across the room, where it lands open a few feet away from the trash.

"Really? Because I'm sure the Eleanor I met didn't write it. This sounds like another version of her. Someone afraid to dream."

"I said it's not mine!" she shouts. "What do you know, anyway? What do you know about fear? Do you know what it's like to be afraid of yourself? To not even be able to trust yourself?"

The question shoots right through me. I feel horrible. I feel mean. Of course I know.

"I'll go," I say, wheeling myself away as fast as I can. I

wheel myself back out into the hall. I wish I could change what I've done. But I can't. And now I'll have to live remembering it.

I'm so sorry. I hate myself. Why do I hurt people? Why can't I fix anything?

But she broke my heart. She hurt me first. She's been fixed. My Eleanor is gone.

✳

When I get back into my room, Lucie is sitting on my bed.

"Sweet wheels," she says, but then she notices I am sniffling. "Bad time? What's wrong?"

"I just want to go home."

"Oh, stop whining. You're coming home in like two days," she says, rummaging around in my drawers. She unearths some of my trinkets from Henry—a stuffed bison, a tiny plastic flamingo—and makes super-gross barfing noises. Normally that makes me laugh. But nothing seems funny.

"I don't know if I'm ever coming home," I say. That stops her.

"What do you mean?"

"I mean I don't know what's wrong with me."

"There's nothing wrong with you."

"No, something is. Something is seriously wrong with

me. Sometimes I feel like I'm pretending to be crazy and if I just tried really hard to be normal . . . all of this would be over. But I can't stop. Isn't that what it means to be crazy?"

"I don't know," she says.

"Can you keep a secret?" I ask her.

"Yeah, of course."

"I was in a car crash right before middle school."

"I know. Everyone knows. You were on the news. I didn't even live here then and people told me. You're basically the girl who lived."

I wince. I think about the opposite: the boy who died.

"But I think . . . maybe it broke something in me. Maybe I didn't live."

Lucie just looks at me and listens.

"I feel like something is wrong, like I'm not supposed to be alive. I can't explain it. It's like the person in me who was special died in the car crash, and I'm the leftover shell."

"What do you mean by special?"

"I don't know," I admit. "I think maybe I just mean alive. I don't feel anything unless I'm reading a book. And I guess I thought if I was in a band or something, like you and Henry, or if I was on an adventure like a character in a story, I would feel alive."

"You can be in the band if you want to," Lucie says quickly. I shake my head.

"No, that's not the point." What would make her understand? I want so much to carry this feeling out of myself and show it to her. I try again: "Sometimes when I was younger, after the crash, I closed my eyes as tight as I could and wished that when I opened them I would be at Hogwarts. And every time, I thought if I only kept my eyes closed one second longer, maybe this would be the time that the wish would come true. I wasn't crazy. I knew it wouldn't happen. I don't know why I did it, but it was my prayer for years. It's what I asked God for every spare second I had."

"Blasphemer!" Lucie shouts in mock outrage. This time I laugh.

"I don't even know if it's really the magic that I love so much. I mean, the magic is amazing, and Quidditch, and the whole world . . . but that's not it. It's something else. Something smaller. It's that a wand can choose you, and a hat can sort you. It's that you are all set up, on the inside, for everything you don't know yet. If you die, you were supposed to die. You died for something. And if there's a prophecy, it comes true. Bad people have bad names, and good people have friendly ones. And everything just . . . works. I don't know. That doesn't make sense."

Lucie nods.

"I guess it's that there's somewhere you belong?" she says hesitantly. "Not like people accept you, but like you have a place, and everyone does. Somewhere you fit, that needs you. Is that what you mean?"

"Yeah. And that everything would be certain, even if you didn't know it yet."

"You want to know that there's destiny."

"Maybe I just want that because then ... my choices don't matter. I wouldn't have to worry so much anymore."

Lucie looks all around her, uncharacteristically silent. Uncomfortable. We sit like that for longer than I've ever heard her quiet before.

"You wanna know something embarrassing?" she asks at last.

"Always."

"I was super-disappointed when I didn't get my Hogwarts letter. Like, legit depressed."

I laugh.

"But I feel like nerding out with you is kind of like going to Hogwarts. You know? You're the only one who will read my fan faction." It is awful. I still love it. "Maybe I don't get exactly what you see in those books. But we kind of meet in the middle, right? We both love the same thing. So maybe that means that I *can* see it. I mean, if you start telling me what's really going on."

"I'm trying. I don't know what to do," I say.

"Maybe you should let your team help you," she says. "Everyone runs their own race, but we are stronger when we run that race together."

Now it's my turn to make terrible gross noises.

"I don't have a team here," I tell her through the laughter.

"We're all your team, stupid! That's what having friends is. Everyone you know is Team Sadie," Lucie says. "God, you are such an idiot."

And it makes me smile: Lucie is my team. For a minute,

it feels like that race that wasn't a race, when we somehow made each other faster just by noticing each other. It feels like getting lost in the present instead of some other world. It is good to have a team, even though you are really alone. And I know she doesn't understand my race. But then, neither do I.

THE ONLY ONE
SHE EVER FEARED

Sadie counted up and down to eleven. She was eleven years old, and counting it gave her a kind of peace. She thought about her life for each of those numbers: how at zero she had known nothing, but at eleven she knew too much. At eleven she knew how to be afraid. Eleven was two straight lines standing tall: constant and unshakable and parallel and good. Just like her parents used to feel. Then she counted back down from eleven and felt all the knowledge and all the trouble fading away. Up and down, up and down in her head.

Her parents were "stable," which was funny because she had only ever heard them being accused of being "unstable." It was unstable to take road trips, to go on adventures, to do a radio show, to have fun. Sadie had liked unstable. Now she wanted nothing more than stability. Sadie sat in the emergency room watching them, fading in and out of the present. The heartbeat monitor kept the moments moving forward, but they were all outside of time. Her parents looked like one of the barely moving photographs in Harry Potter. She imagined them stranded in this moment for all eternity.

Sadie felt a hand on her shoulder, ruining the illusion of stillness. These moments were happening. Who knew what the next moment would bring? She looked up. When she looked back on this day years later, she could remember everything about the scenes that made up the story except the faces. Later, her mind injected George into all her memories, the most comforting face she could think of.

"Your grandparents are coming," the man wearing George's face said. "Would you like to stay here?"

Sadie nodded.

"Everything is going to be all right," he said, and he walked away.

But nothing would be all right. Everything had changed.

Her grandparents came and picked her up, and she was, according to them, miraculously unscathed.

"That must have been so scary," they said.

"I don't know," Sadie replied. "I don't remember a thing."

"But that wasn't true?" asked Dr. Roberts, and Sadie was sixteen and it was the present again and she wasn't in the story, she was *telling* the story. She was back in the horrible confrontation of *now,* two crashes becoming one.

She'd said she was ready to talk about this.

She wasn't. But she never would be. So she kept moving forward anyway.

"No," she said quietly. "It wasn't."

She remembered the first crash, the long hours in the car upside down, which she'd been told had only been minutes. It didn't matter. Time had come undone. She remembered how her parents had been in the front seat, bloody and unseeing, bent at unnatural angles into airbags. She remembered the sound of sirens, the smell of gasoline, the Beatles singing, strangely, to the beat of the seat belt warning sound.

A car and their truck had landed upside down side by side, smashed up next to each other. She remembered the other driver crying: "Please help me. I don't want to die."

"I'm sorry. I'm sorry," Sadie whispered.

In her memories, the other driver too was played by George: George, who could never die, who would stand up and take a bow at the end of every episode.

But when she tried—when she *really* tried—she could remember the boy's real face: his brown eyes, his hair so matted with blood she couldn't tell what color it was. She could picture his mouth hanging open, screaming and dribbling blood outside her window. The dignified, dressed wounds of film heroes were nothing like this. The boy was soaked in a burnt black gore she could smell. This was no stage makeup. He was unraveling in the car beside her, right through the frame of the broken window, and whoever he had been, he was not going to be that person for long.

Who had he been? She would never know. But she was the only one who knew those moments. They only existed because she remembered.

She couldn't stop remembering.

Sadie, at sixteen, was back in the truck again. She could never get away from this day. The crash drew her back to Day Zero, the bomb blast that shattered her entire life.

The moments passed, every one a framed photo to look at safely from where she sat. She knew it wasn't happening, she was just replaying it again.

And again, she was eleven. She lived through it again: her milk shake splashed against the roof of the car, pooling in her hair, and how it was still hot and summery. How she still thought about the weather even while people were dying. The humidity was terrible. The ceiling was covered in blue broken glass diamonds, glittering like stars in the sky.

She replayed it again, and again, and again. Her parents, shouting. The other car. The crash. The waiting. Again. And again. And again.

She remembered knowing that she was alone, utterly and completely alone, without control. And she whispered to herself:

> I'm not here
>   I'm not here
>   I'm not here
>   I'm not here. . . .

She stared up at the stars, which were made of broken blue safety glass on the roof of the car. Her hair was floating, like she was underwater. She was sixteen and eleven, outside of time. She looked into the sky of stars that she had imagined and saw George—her George, in his royal white jacket and pure white gloves—beckoning. She reached up and took his hand.

And off to the Star Palace she went.

✳

"Sadie?" called Dr. Roberts, snatching her back to reality. The verdant garden smell became bleach and latex. Sadie shook her head, and she was in the hospital again.

"Yeah?"

"Why didn't you tell anyone what you remembered?"

Sadie shrugged, and George paced nervously behind her.

"She's asking too many questions," George said. "You know this is getting too dangerous."

"I just didn't," Sadie said. But it wasn't that simple. She hadn't wanted to remember herself.

"Does this have to do with George?"

Sadie looked away.

"You mean the other driver," Sadie said quietly.

"Is there another George?"

"There's . . . my George," Sadie said. But then she was thinking about the first George: no more than a teenager. He had said, "Please help me. I don't want to die," until he didn't say anything else. She knew he wasn't talking to her, but to no one, because he was alone too. All alone, with no one to help him.

They were all like that. Her parents, herself. Trapped together, completely alone.

And the whole time she heard The Tape going on and on and on . . . *Blackbird fly . . . Blackbird fly . . .*

"Sadie!" Dr. Roberts called, but Sadie didn't answer. "What happened that day wasn't your fault. Maybe it's time to let George go."

"I can't. . . . I love him," Sadie said. George put his head in his hands.

"Sadie, who in the world are you talking about?" Roberts asked.

"George."

"Sadie, I'm confused. You didn't know George. Are you talking about the other driver, or someone else?"

Sadie closed her eyes so the world wouldn't vanish.

"I want my parents," Sadie said softly. "Where are they?"

"Sadie, please. Please don't," said George.

"I need help," Sadie told him. "I'm trapped and all alone."

✳

Sadie wheeled herself down to the cafeteria and found her parents sitting at a table, their accounting all spread out around them. They'd been working for hours.

"Can I talk to you?" Sadie asked, surprising them. They had an extended eyeball conversation that Sadie could not interpret, but she said: "It's important."

"Of course," said her dad. "Even if it's *not* important, you can tell us anything."

As she gathered all her strength, the cafeteria became the ER from the first crash, and her parents were back in their beds, bloodied to within an inch of their lives but somehow listening to her. She couldn't keep it straight. She was sixteen and eleven, falling in and out of time.

"Do you remember the crash?" Sadie asked. Her parents fidgeted with their IVs and bandages, like actors in a hospital scene. They weren't really hurt, in this memory. It was all pretend.

"I don't really," her mom said. "It never came back to me after the accident."

"Me neither," her dad said.

"So you don't know what caused it." Sadie sighed. She could feel the truth raging to be let go. She tried to say it. Instead, she relived it.

They were all exhausted at the end of a long drive.

She saw her parents in the front seat, and she felt herself saying their names over and over because they weren't listening. She wanted to hear The Tape. She felt a rage she couldn't explain, being strapped into the backseat for hours and hours, ignored. She was trying to behave.

The Tape was in the stereo already. All they had to do was press play. It had seemed so simple. She just wanted to listen to it.

Her mom was saying, "No, just wait," and "Sadie, stop, we're driving," and looking into the backseat, and her dad was saying, "Okay, just quiet down," as he pressed play and then he was yelling and Old Charlotte slammed headfirst into a green Honda Civic.

"You were distracted because I wanted to listen to my Beatles tape," Sadie admitted.

"No, Sadie, that's not what happened. We've talked about this. The other driver wasn't paying attention. He was in our lane." Her mom was so certain that Sadie almost believed her.

"No, I remember what happened."

"You always said you didn't remember anything."

"I remember every day," Sadie confessed. "Trying not to remember is remembering."

"The accident didn't happen because of your tape. You didn't know how to drive. How would you have known who was in the right?" her dad asked.

"But it doesn't matter. If you'd been paying attention you might have gotten out of the way! It was my fault all this happened. I killed that other driver. You know he was only eighteen?"

"Of course we know that. You probably don't remember all the legal stuff, all issues with the insurance. We know a lot about him," her mom said. She hesitated. "His name was—"

"George," Sadie said. "I know."

"That's right. How did you know that?"

"Because it was on the news. You can look it up in the paper. Everyone knows. I heard him, when we were in the car. Before the ambulances came. He was crying and crying and crying. No one heard. No one remembers but me. No one else knows what really happened. I have to carry it forever."

"Stop, Sadie. Before it's too late," George begged. But she couldn't stop. She saw his face on every nurse, every doctor, every patient, every relative who had been in the ER that terrible day. The ceiling disappeared and became a starry night, just like the ceiling of the Star Palace rising above. The ER ground to a halt around them, and all these Georges watched as she betrayed him.

"Sometimes I wonder if maybe we all died," she said, choking on tears. "I worry until I make myself sick. Or maybe just I died and that's why I don't feel anything. And I play that day in my head over and over and over and over and over and I wish I hadn't been asking for my tape and I wish you hadn't been arguing and I wish and I wish and I wish and nothing changes. *Nothing* changes. I've told myself this story a million times and nothing changes."

"Sadie, nothing can change the past," her dad said. "And it's not a story. It's a terrifying thing that happened to us. And to that boy."

"That must have been frightening for you, being awake in the car after the crash. It must have been horrifying." Her mom wiped away a few tears, choking on her words before she could continue. "I can hardly bear to think about it. But you know, it was an accident. It was an accident and we're all okay now."

"But the other driver died."

"He did," her mom admitted, but there wasn't anything she could say to make that better. They sat in silence.

"But we're okay now," her dad said finally.

"Don't you get it? Don't you understand? Everything can fall down in an instant. You can't control anything. And then you have to wonder, is it fate or could we have changed it? I ask over and over, could it have been different? Life only goes one direction, and this moment, and the next moment, once they're in the past you can't change them and there's no reason for anything that happens. You can't stop time and it paralyzes me. I mean, what if we hadn't been okay? What if?"

"But that didn't happen," her mom said. "What happened, happened. And here we are."

"And it was scary. Tragic," her dad added. "But everything is okay now."

"Nothing is okay," Sadie said, putting her head in her hands. "And I don't know why."

"What do you mean?" her mom asked.

"Nothing feels real," Sadie mumbled. "I feel empty and worthless and cold. All the time. And no one sees. I feel like a ghost. Like I'm just pretending to be alive. I don't even know if it was the accident or if I just am this way. There's no reason for it. But I think there should be a reason for everything and there isn't. I don't get why I have to be this sad. I don't know."

Sadie's parents looked at each other, but their telepathic conversation seemed to fail them.

Sadie stared up at the ceiling she knew so well: the Star Palace's beautiful glass false sky. Here in the real world, to real people, she couldn't explain what it felt like. Words could never carry the shattered feeling she lived with out of her body and into another mind.

Only George knew how she really felt. His many hospital guises stood like a jury around her.

"They'll never understand," all the Georges said at once.

"I don't understand!" I shouted back.

I shouted. Me.

I looked up, but I had to cover my eyes. It was blinding.

The shattering roof made horrible music. All around me, broken glass stars were falling. The palace roof was falling down, abandoning me to reality in a shower of stars. They burned bright as they died, a thousand wishes going out.

The soft bustle of the hospital cafeteria began again, and my parents were looking at me, shocked.

Because I was there, suddenly. In a way that I'm usually not. I was there despite the darkness that had taken over, through the dreaming, in the real world. My words were like the staff that strikes the water, parting the sea. Magic, powerful words.

"I need help. I really, really need someone to help me," I sobbed, and they put their arms around me, sheltering me from the black water that was already coming back, that too-familiar cold.

"It's okay," my parents said over and over as I sank back into the ocean of sadness, and I knew they just didn't know what else to say. "Sadie. We're here."

DAY 13

How can such a world-destroying whirlwind exist in a span of twelve days? You can create a world in seven, I guess. We used to go to church for Grandma and Grandpa's sake, and Mom used to say Genesis was a metaphor: a device to tell the story, to make a point. The right story can be more true than the truth. Why is that?

But then, stories can also lie.

I don't know how to sort out the difference between a true story and a story that lies, when no one ever has the *whole* story. If you can't trust your memory, what can you trust? I don't know how anyone is ever certain about anything.

I am writing the truth in my journal, and it's building a storm of words I can barely see through. Some are just fragments; others are thoughts I've been holding in for too long. At the heart of the storm is the truth I know already, though I can't write it down, and when the center falls, all the scary beautiful magic I've been building will fall too.

It isn't a perfect metaphor, I think. The eye doesn't cause the storm. It is the consequence of it. You have to let the storm die out to free what is at its center.

How long have I been living in this tempest? It's time to go home.

My mom walks in just as I'm writing that, sneaking up on me while I'm lost in thought. Today I don't mind, though. Maybe it's okay if she sees my funny thinking faces.

She's got a couple of our old suitcases we haven't used in forever. She's taking home half of my stuff today, because tomorrow I'm getting out of here (for real this time). Between Henry and my mom and my team, we brought so much stuff into this hospital that she wasn't sure she could take it all at once.

She sits down on my bed and puts a book-sized present in front of me wrapped up in pretty pink paper.

"I know you know you didn't cause that crash," she says. "But I also know that maybe it feels like you did."

"Yeah," I say.

"I do think I remember a little. For some reason, all those old Beatles albums gave me a chill. I never knew why. But you messing around with the tape player didn't cause the accident."

"I guess."

"But it's not just the accident, is it?" she says. I shake my head. "Sadie, I don't understand what you're trying to tell us. I don't understand what's wrong. But I want to."

"I don't know if you can," I say. "I don't know if it was the crash or if I'm just blaming everything on the worst thing that ever happened. But since then, I've been broken in a million pieces. Everything seemed wrong after that."

My mom nods. "Well, you started going to school, and we started a whole new life. And that was partly the crash, and partly just because things change. It's hard to figure out who you are when life hands you a new adventure."

"A consolation prize."

She scoffs.

"I know you liked being on the road. All those 'road years,' like you used to say. But you don't remember how hard it was, pulling together a living that way. All you remember is the fun parts. And we're glad you do; there were a lot of them. But I don't think that this life, the one we ended up with, was a consolation prize at all. Sadie, we *chose* this. It wasn't forced on us. We took what happened, and we made a choice as a family, and we moved on. You were part of that choice."

"But everything . . . broke," I say. I don't know how better to say it. Our whole lives, my sense of certainty, my future . . .

"I don't believe in broken. Neither does your dad. But I do believe in change. Do you remember, when you were little, we were at a museum and there was all this Japanese art and pottery? I don't even remember if it was Chicago or Detroit. One of those long trips. There were so many they just blend together.

"There was this blue cup you absolutely loved. It had been broken and sort of glued back together with gold. It was amazing, because it was so beautiful after it had been broken. And I felt stupid liking this cup that was such an obvious metaphor: that the cracks made it stronger and more beautiful." She swats me gently. "I can see you rolling your eyes, you smart aleck." I laugh a little. "I mean, it's trite. But now I think about it sometimes and I like it. Because sometimes the truth really is just completely cliché. And I think this is one of those times. There is beauty in fixing something. There's beauty in restoration. And there's room for broken things to be better than they were before."

"That is super-sappy," I admit. "But I like it too."

"Anyway," she says. "This is for you. Because you're not a ghost. You're someone special and your story is just beginning."

I open it. It is a beautiful leather-bound journal exactly like an explorer would have.

"Thank you," I say.

"And your dad is taking the Beatles records out of the basement as we speak," my mom says. "We're on a huge nostalgia kick, and you can't beat vinyl."

"That's what Henry says."

"Henry knows a good thing when he sees it."

She kisses me and leaves. There's nothing more to say,

nothing she could tell me that would make me happier than
that. I repeat it to myself, rearranging it. "I am a good thing,
seen." I want to write those words down in my new journal, but when I open it and face those blank cream-white
pages, I realize I'm not done with this story yet. So, I take
out the battered green one, flip past the mess of thoughts
I've scribbled today, and think of the true things I know.

I think I love old things because I want to know the ending before I start. I love the Beatles because they're already
over. There can't be any more. No one can make a new Beatles song. There are no surprises and you are safe. That's
why it hurts so much to discover:

You can always add meaning to something, even if it's in the
past. A tape playing during an accident becomes a memory, and
the song means something new.

Of course, I think, *that isn't always a bad thing.*

What is a cover? Somewhere between an old song and a
new one. Everything builds on everything else. Stories never die.
There really isn't an end.

My story, the one that's in this notebook with its cracked
green cover and tearstained pages, is a red and black mess of
lines. It's not even really a story. It's just facts I wish weren't
true. Boring, mundane existence on cheap paper. It's fragments. I flip into the very front and look at Day 1: a few

sentences. It isn't the whole truth, with all the depth and complexity of living through it. It's just what I thought were "facts." It's embarrassing to be distilled down into so few words, and for those words to be . . . nothing. Boring. But in a way, that's the truth too. I've been writing the truth all along.

I sit in my wheelchair in the bathroom crumpling a section in my fist, ready to tear it out and pretend that all this never happened. None of this. *Just rip it up and throw it away and it will be gone.* If I leave all these words here in the hospital, I'll be free of them, and eventually I will forget that they were ever more permanent than a passing thought.

Why did I write any of this down? I made it real. I'm the one who's killing George, after all.

My fist clenches, but I don't throw it away. I can't. Trying not to remember is remembering. So you have to remember. Even if it's embarrassing. Even if it's true.

The thing is, though, facts can say a lot of things. You choose where the story starts and ends, and what lines you draw between the things that are true. You can tell a lot of stories with the same facts. I thought I knew what story I was telling. Now I'm not so sure.

I smooth out the pages and start looking through them. So much is changing. Maybe leaving a hospital is always like that. Your world is destroyed on the way in and re-created on the way out. I'm going home and everything is different.

And . . .

I think I want it to be.

THE FINAL HIDING PLACE

Knowing what she had to do didn't make it any easier. Sadie stood at the window for a long time, her feet cold on the linoleum floor. It would be so easy to hide George in the Antarctic, in a distant kingdom, even at Hogwarts. It would be so easy to lock him up safe in the Star Palace, tell a few lies, and be on her way. She had the strength to do it.

She gathered all her bravery and summoned him into the lucid night.

George came reluctantly, with wilting red flowers. He handed them to her with downcast eyes.

"I tried to find better ones," he said.

"They're perfect." Sadie put them on the nightstand, and as soon as her hand left them, they turned to dust.

"Everything is getting weaker," he explained. "It's been hard."

Sadie held him close. He was hardly dust. He smelled like he always did: an innocent's dream of bourbon and smoke. He felt so real.

"Are you angry?" she asked into his white shirt.

"No, darling. Only a little sad."

He wrapped her in his arms. It was such a relief, like being closed in by a tree that would last a thousand years. She imagined the rings of wood encasing her, building her in for eternity in the complete embrace of George.

She realized her face was wet, so she pulled away, wiping her cheek. Her hand came away red.

"Why are you bleeding?" She felt the panic rise.

"You're killing me, Sadie." He put her hand over the wound, and she closed it with magic that seemed harder and harder to control. She could heal him or destroy him in an instant.

"Oh, George. What are we going to do?"

"Can we leave?" George asked. Sadie nodded and took his hand. Effortlessly, they were gone.

✳

They crept slowly down the long hallway in their museum of memories, where the once-grand dioramas had succumbed to ruin. Portraits hung ripped to shreds. The cafeteria was full of food that had hardened to plates. The lights flickered and threatened to die. It only got worse as they journeyed closer to the palace. Every step drew them deeper into decay.

They rushed along the now dingy celestial patterns in the floor, barely distracted by all the wonders that had tempted them before. They passed an Aston Martin—the one Sadie had always coveted—under a spotlight in a circle of red velvet ropes. "Come on, it might be faster," George said, climbing in and turning the key. The whole car shuddered and fell to pieces.

"What happens to all this?" Sadie asked as she helped him out of the wreckage.

"Anything can be fixed. That's what your dad always says."

A painting of George's victory over the basilisk fell down with a deafening crack, startling them both. They moved along at a brisker step.

Before, the museum had conspired against them, every twist and turn leading them away from the star on the map. Now they seemed to fly across continents of memory. In no time at all they'd nearly made it to the place where the map claimed the palace would stand, though Sadie had begun to lose hope that it would still be there. So deep in, even the walls had started to fall, and the palace was nowhere in sight.

"Wait," George said suddenly, darting off into a side room. "Come here," he called.

"George, the whole building could come down. We have to hurry."

"But look. It's what I wanted to show you last time."

Sadie looked into the room. The roof was missing, and a cold night wind blew in from above. There was a storm outside, snow fluttering into the room. On a pedestal, she saw herself in elementary school wearing a princess costume she'd once worn for Halloween with a witch's hat. She didn't look real. She looked like a ballerina in a music box.

"Don't you remember? On The Tape? 'You've Got to Hide Your Love Away' is in waltz time. That's when I first taught you how to waltz," George said. Sadie watched herself twirling with her Walkman in her hand, a ghost of George in his prince's white coat and gloves towering over her, dancing with her.

"But we're not waltzing," Sadie pointed out. It was true. They weren't even remotely in time.

"But you *thought* you were. To you, we were. To me, we were. In our heads, we were perfect. You just can't see it anymore because . . ."

"Because what?"

"I'm worried that it might already be too late."

She looked again at the scene, trying to see the magic. Something wasn't right.

"We didn't even know each other then," Sadie said.

"Don't you see, Sadie? It's always been me. Even before you knew it was me, even before you gave me a name, I was every dream you ever had."

Like a shadow of a song carried by the wind, Sadie could hear "You've Got to Hide Your Love Away" very faintly. He continued:

"I am every prince, every song, every car, every street. I am not just me. I'm in everything you've built. And this, here, is the monument to all you have created. To me. To you. This is the Museum of Us."

The music rose. When she looked again, she saw not a dingy costume but a flowing gown.

"This place is our lives, our stories, and everything that means something to you. It's the *true world,* Sadie. That's what this museum protects. And if you let it fall apart, and the Star Palace at its center falls ... then that true world will be gone too. That is what is at stake. Darling, you must understand. This is what you stand to lose."

All of a sudden, thunder cracked and the storm outside the museum flooded the room with snow. It was so cold she could barely breathe. George grabbed her hand and they ran to safety. The walls caved in behind them, closing off the room entirely.

"Did you see?" he asked desperately. Sadie didn't answer. They had to get to the Star Palace. They needed sanctuary. They needed time to sort this out.

"Come on," she said, helping him up, leaving the destruction behind them. "The star on the map should be just around the corner."

※

"This must be the entrance," George said, his fingers tracing thorny letters. The point on the map where the palace was meant to be was no more than a tiny door of wrought silver. The little branches that made up the frame entwined themselves in the center to form words: TO SEEK AND FIND.

Sadie twisted the handle. It gave little resistance and swung open.

Behind the door was not the Star Palace's great lawn, with its magnificent gardens of impossible flowers. Not the ballroom with its glass ceiling and celestial floors, of which the museum's were a dull imitation. It wasn't even her bedroom at the palace, with its canopy bed under a cascade of velvet and its great marble balcony with its view of planet Earth and the moon. It was only her bedroom in the basement at home.

They squeezed themselves through the door.

"Well, this is a surprise," George said, sitting at the desk. He tapped some keys on the computer and it sprang to life. Google Maps was up, exactly as it was when she'd left. The floor was still littered with markers and purloined atlases.

"Why did the map say the palace was here?" Sadie asked. She unfurled one of the maps on the floor: one of their red Sharpie plans. She could see the little bend in the park where they'd gone into the tree. She pulled the lid off a Sharpie and drew an X over the spot: the zero point.

She jumped back as two figures appeared on the floor, thin and hollow as fog. George caught her and she braced herself against him.

"It's us," George said, inspecting the unseeing ghosts.

"It's us before we left." Sadie recognized the pajamas she'd worn the night before the crash. The memory chilled her. She went to the door they'd come through, but it was locked. She looked desperately at George. There weren't any windows. They were trapped.

The ghost of Sadie-two-weeks-ago was lying facedown on the floor in her pajamas, her eyes closed, neither awake nor asleep. In the present, Sadie could remember clearly the feeling of carpet on her cheek, how the pain of that felt almost pleasant.

"I don't want to see this," present-Sadie said to George.

"I don't think we have a choice. This is the last monster to slay before we make it through the door."

"How are we slaying it?"

"By seeing it how it really was."

So they kept their eyes open, and they watched as the truth unfurled before them in ghostly wisps of fog:

"Let's go outside." George paced the floor, stepping over Sadie's unmoving arm. She didn't say anything.

"Well, we can't just sit down here all night," he continued. "Don't you want to go for a walk? It'll clear your mind. Then we can go——"

"George, I don't want to go anywhere," she said softly.

Tears fell down the sides of her face. She had her hand resting on a book but she couldn't even read it. She just wanted to sleep.

She'd seen her parents off for their red-eye, then come downstairs. For a moment, the thrill of being alone had been exciting. But she'd passed the itinerary they'd left for her and felt the noose of her life closing around her. She was free, but she wasn't. She started receding into her own mind past George and into darkness.

She glanced at an empty bottle of pills on the bureau. She'd grabbed it from her parents' bathroom to use as a prop in a fantasy. There'd been a lot of prescriptions in the house since the crash, forgotten in cabinets and drawers, pills of all shapes and sizes. The sight of them now sickened her, making her think of the overturned car and the screaming. Her whole mind shut down just to avoid it.

"Come on," George said.

"I just want to sleep."

"No you don't. We haven't gone anywhere for so long. We've been down in this room for a week. You just put on your mask for your parents and then sleep all the time."

"It doesn't matter anyway. No one sees anything about anyone. No one really notices."

"Then no one will notice if we're gone on an adventure! There's no mask to wear: it's just us! Let's go sneak out to U City! Come on, your parents are on their plane already."

"Just leave me alone," Sadie said. The words came out slowly. Even speaking had begun to feel like a weight on her chest.

"I bet Lucie's up for a night out," he said. She didn't answer. She was supposed to go to Lucie's in the afternoon the next day and stay for a week. She wasn't sure she could keep her normal person act up for that long.

George shuffled around, thumbing through books they'd read. When was the last time they'd been awake enough to read a book? He sighed, then ventured reluctantly:

"What about Henry?"

"You hate Henry. And anyway, he's not even in town."

"You could call him," George said, grabbing her phone and pushing it under her fingers. She curled into a ball on the floor, turning her back on it.

"What's the point?"

"Sadie, can't we go on an adventure?"

" 'To die will be an awfully big adventure,' " she said, quoting Peter Pan. The usual flourish with which she delivered this line sounded dim.

George gritted his teeth. "Sadie. That's not funny."

"Do you think if I died, we could be together?"

"No," George said. He followed Sadie's eyes to the empty pill bottle on the bureau. He put it into his pocket. "No, I'm pretty sure we'd never see each other again. And I like being alive. And I like you being alive. So let's not even talk like that."

George shuffled nervously, then sat down on the floor next to her. He hesitated, then kissed her.

"Stop it," she said with a sigh. "Please just leave me alone. I'm so tired."

"I don't know how to make you happy."

"Neither do I."

Her eyes were closed. She turned away, and instead of carpet, she landed nose-first on a pile of oversized maps. George stood over her, looking down into the greens and blues of other countries.

"I have an idea. Let me give you one perfect day," George said. He pushed her aside, jolting her awake. She sat up and watched as he started scribbling in red Sharpie on the map, drawing in all the places they would go. Sadie looked at the snaking lines: the park, ice cream, her favorite diner, the zoo, the museum . . . and home again.

"That's just all around town."

"It'll be more than that. Look: All our favorite things. A whole day, just you and me. Let me show you how magic I can make the world."

She looked at it again. It was almost a square.

"It's a red frame," she said. "Boxing us in."

"No, it's . . ." He struggled to come up with something. "It's a bright red line toward destiny. Just because it ends where it started doesn't make it any less of a path. You see a trap. I see an adventure!"

"But it won't be real."

"How? You'll really be there. I'll be with you. I promise, this will be an adventure." He capped the pen and pointed dramatically at the map. "Let's do something amazing. You've got a hundred pictures here of adventures you wanted to have with me. Maybe if we just go on those adventures, you won't feel so . . ."

"Feel so what?"

"I don't know what's happened to you. But I know that we were happier before. All you have to do is take the first step. I'll carry us the rest of the way. An all-new exploration. A brand-new frontier. Come on, Sadie—to seek and find."

"To seek and find . . . ," Sadie repeated.

And with that, the ghosts faded and were gone.

Sadie almost couldn't bear to look over at George, who

had been ruined by that fateful trip. He was inspecting his shoes.

"George—"

"Do we have to talk about this?"

"George, we can't keep orbiting it."

"I just wanted to help."

Before she could say more, they noticed: the closet was glowing. The light from beyond the door was celestial, familiar. It glittered and beckoned. When they opened the door, it was not Sadie's disaster of a closet at all, but the long green hill up to the Star Palace at last. It was completely overgrown with thicket and thorns.

✳

The great door to the palace was sealed with vines. George removed his sword from his belt and hacked away at them.

"It's abandoned," Sadie said.

"No, just . . . a little . . . overgrown," George grunted between thwacks with his sword. Sadie placed her hands on the vines, whispering a spell. They withered away, but in their death throes strangled the door even tighter. George sliced through the dead vines and managed to pull open the door just enough for them to slip through.

"Is my obsession with dark things locked behind doors too psychologically transparent?" Sadie asked as she pushed herself through the tiny entry.

"Not in the least. The real world is full of doors too."

George stood in the booming, echoing great hall, looking up at their decrepit home. Bats, disturbed by their entrance, fluttered across the shattered ceiling. So the ceiling really was destroyed, she thought. Sadie stood beside him looking at what remained of the glass above.

George reached for her and she hesitated. "Come on. The lights don't work either."

"That seems too poetic."

"It's dark, darling. Just take my hand."

She did. Even in the dark, she could feel him grin.

Upstairs, the blood-red carpet led to the tower, which had the best view of heaven and earth. It held their bedroom, the heart of the palace. When they reached the door, they were grateful to find it unlocked. George stepped into the room over a pile of mangled picture frames. He lifted her easily over the mess. A cold wind blew through the window and the door slammed behind them.

"There, see? Everything is still here. It just needs some cleaning up," George said, gathering fallen mementos and broken pictures in his arms. He opened a trunk to dump them inside but instead set them on the floor and gazed into the trunk.

"What is it?" Sadie asked. He reached in and held up his white jacket.

"Do you remember when this was all you wanted? All you needed to be truly happy?" George asked, putting the old costume on: white jacket and gloves, hair swept back. He closed the jacket carefully, looking at himself in the tall mirror. The gold braid had frayed, knots of it crossing his chest.

She couldn't help but smile. George looked at her in the reflection.

"But I guess you think that wasn't *true* happiness," he said. "It wasn't *real.*"

"I was happy. I had you."

"Well. *Have,*" he said. "Not *had* yet."

He pulled at the fingers of one glove, one at a time, then removed the other one. He laid the gloves to rest back in the trunk. He began to take off the jacket. Sadie felt her arm reach out and put one hand on the twists of gold. Beneath her fingers, they glimmered and twisted into their original brilliance, all the dinginess of time coming off the white coat.

He wrapped his bare hands around hers, clutching them to his heart. A little of the color came back into his cheeks.

"Don't you think you owe me some kind of reality?" he mumbled. He couldn't look at her.

"You're not real," Sadie said gently. She pulled her hands away.

"I was to you," he pleaded. "I matter. I feel. I deserve an ending, at least. Sadie, I love you."

"You're not real," she repeated, this time to herself.

"God damn it!" he yelled, punching the mirror. It shattered and fell to the floor. He jumped back, frightened of his own anger. He turned on her. "Don't you see? This is exactly what I warned you about! They've tricked you. They've stolen your dreams. Think, Sadie. Try to remember. Of *course* I'm not real. But to you, to me . . . this matters. The mattering is what's real. This is what's been keeping you alive. And you're just going to let that die."

"George. You are a symptom."

"That's not true."

"It *is*. You are a sickness, and it's time for me to get better. That's what I'm supposed to say, right?"

George leaned against the silver balcony, looking out over his shoulder at the stars. They seemed so close.

"The sickness is the *world,* Sadie. Why does it have to be so black-and-white? Why is it either real or me? Stories are special. Powerful. Stories make sense of what reality leaves as absolute chaos. Constellations arrange themselves out of meaningless stars. The universe aligns in the translation of moments into story.

"That's the magic of fiction: that something can be more true than the truth. That's the magic of you and me. Why would you want to throw that away?"

"Because . . . we can't unsee. We can't unlearn. We can't ungrow. George, what I wanted more than *anything* was to be with you. But now everything's broken open and in the light. I have to live in the real world. We can't go back. There's only forward."

George paced, the way he did when he came close to losing at chess, even though he always beat Sadie in the end.

"Listen," he tried again. "You can't be a wizard in the real world. You can't be a spy in the real world. You can't have this great and timeless love. If you choose to be *only* real, Sadie, there is so much you will never do. And Henry's great, but he's not me. No one ever will be. You know it's true. Real isn't what you want."

"How am I supposed to know what I want when I spend all my time with you?"

"Alternative hypothesis: you know what you want. That's *why* we spend all of our time together."

Sadie sighed and walked to the balcony.

It was an impossible choice.

It would be so easy to keep him safe. No one really knew her thoughts, not even Henry. She could hide George away, tell Roberts just enough to get out, and be more careful next time to never let him show. Maybe she could even admit that George wasn't real. *Could I tell a lie that big, and bring him back?* she wondered. She looked around. Of course she could. If she could dream a story this big, she could dream anything.

The temptation was there, glinting in George's eyes. She could pretend that she'd exiled him from her mind. She didn't have to let all of this go.

She leaned over and looked into the abyss below, into the distant planet with all its blue oceans and green land, its moon on the other side, still a sliver rising. The earth was an infinitely complex machine of particles floating along a defined orbit. On its surface, how many protagonists were starring in their own little dramas? And what did it matter if in one little hospital in one little city, one little girl was dreaming all of this?

Why was that so wrong?

DAY 14

Research and books can tell you almost anything, but they can't tell you *everything*. Sometimes you need to talk to someone.

I take out my earbuds and smile at my tiny iPod shuffle: Henry's mixtape. It doesn't tell you what the songs are, so it's both magic and maddening. I hate not knowing things. I can pick his songs out of a million, I'm certain, but a few others I don't recognize, so I take out my new phone, which is clean and empty of text messages and history, and send the first new text.

"Addicted to this cover," I text Henry.

"Which?" he texts back a millisecond later.

"Guitar torture version of 'As Time Goes By.'"

"LOL guitar torture?!"

"Who is it?"

"These punk twin girls I met this summer. They might come tour with us next year. You'll really like them; they're almost as cool as you."

(Note the semicolon. Next time he asks me, I'm adding this to my list of reasons why I love him.)

"Next summer?" I text after a minute.

"Emoji heart." He always writes out emojis. Reason #2 of the day.

I reply: "Emoji heart emoji heart."

And then, my fingers shaking, I find the letters to write: "Would you record a cover for me? There's a Beatles song I want to hear you sing."

At the door I hear a soft knock. My phone buzzes again, but I shove it into my pocket before I see Henry's reply.

The door opens.

My dad puts the toe of his shoe over the threshold and stops. "Hi," he mumbles.

"Hi," I reply. He looks like he hasn't slept in two weeks. The eternal grease living under his nails has been scrubbed, but his eyes are blackout tired. And I realize I really don't know what me being here has been like for him and Mom. What were they doing all this time?

"We're a little early," he says.

"Where's Mom?"

"Getting coffee."

"Can I have some?"

"If it's decaf."

"*Dad.*" He laughs, and some of the weariness is crossed out by the smile lines on his face.

"Fine, you win. I'll text her." He pulls out his phone and it feels like an excuse not to look at me. But you can only play with a phone for so long, and then you're back in reality.

He slides it back into his pocket. We stare at each other like a paused movie.

"How are you?" he asks, rolling and unrolling his shirtsleeves. His eyes pick over the room, looking at what's left of the treasures I have accumulated in such a short time. His gaze seems to rest on the notebook on the bed.

"Fine," I say, sliding the notebook into my lap. I need my book of truth and secrets for what comes next. I've been writing in it all night.

"Okay." He opens his mouth to say more, but nothing comes out.

He's scared. I see that. But I'm scared too.

Is this the silence we're going back to? Is this the noose of unspoken things growing tighter? The drums in my chest hit a crescendo, like the soundtrack telling me to flee. Ever a coward, I obey.

"I have to go," I tell him, wheeling myself out the door and putting him behind me. "I'll be back after."

"We saw a great Aston Martin on the way here," he calls out to my back as I roll away. "Some kind of classic car club or something meeting in the park. I was thinking maybe we could stop and ask around. . . . Maybe someone's got a junker just like Old Charlotte."

I turn my wheelchair to face him.

"We can't bring back Old Charlotte. She's gone," I say. His eyes fall. "But I would take an Aston Martin."

He laughs. "Keep dreaming, Sadie."

"I'd like to look, though," I add. "Maybe not today. I kind of want to go home. But sometime."

He smiles and his eyes brighten. "Any time you want."

✳

I roll myself into Dr. Roberts's office, and she's standing by her shelves. I wonder if she planned it that way: that she'd be standing there with her back to the door, hands behind her back, gazing at the spines of her books. When I come in she turns around and smiles, and she sets a little plastic cup right on the desk in front of me.

"Hi," I say, because it's all too much. I am taken over by that sense of strangeness, like I could draw a square around the limits of the scene, framing it. So instead I think about real things: about the nurses in the hall and how they all have a sense of style even in scrubs. I think about what the scribbles on the whiteboards on the doors are for. I think about what Henry is doing at exactly this moment, exactly right now. And Lucie. I think about Eleanor, wherever she is.

"Ready to get out of here? Bet you're tired of hospital food," Roberts says.

"Can I see Eleanor before I leave?"

"Eleanor's gone home," she says. "She didn't say good-bye?"

I cross my arms and she smiles, like she's read some kind of super-secret meaning in that body language. So I uncross my arms and glare at her, but she keeps smiling. She opens up my folder and flips through some pages. My folder has gotten pretty thick. An encyclopedia, an epic of notes about me, telling my story. I clutch my journal tight. My version of that story is thinner, but maybe it's more true because it's mine.

I remember what Eleanor told me, about how dangerous these people really are.

But I don't feel that way. Not really.

"Great. Well, let's see. . . . We agreed that we'd start with an antidepressant. . . ."

"Wait, don't you want to . . . ?"

"Yes?"

"Talk."

"About what?" Her eyes light up.

"About . . ."

"George?"

"Yeah," I say.

"You want to tell me about George?"

"Which George?"

She doesn't look stunned the way I expect her to. She just waits. The silence wants my secrets, and I want to fill it.

"Because, you see, there are at least two of them: my George, and the George you're talking about, who was in the other car, who changed everything in one accidental moment. That's not my George, but he's a George."

"Your George is . . . ?"

"My George is . . ." I try to think, but there are too many

words flying around in my head. "My George is a million people . . . an infinity of options. . . ."

"But who is he?" she presses.

I try to say, but all my words flutter away.

I open my journal in my lap. Toward the end, I find the pages that are completely written over, sentences toppling over sentences, memories intersecting memories. The page looks like a black storm of words.

I look at the truth. I've written it right there in the middle of the page: three words in one bright white eye, the center of a hurricane of text. I cannot say them out loud, but I must. I let the words lift themselves off the page, possess me, and speak themselves with my mouth:

George isn't real.

Dr. Roberts's eyes twinkle. She doesn't miss a step. Did she know all along?

"Ah. And you see, this is the question we must ponder. Because . . . we're still talking about him like he's real. He seems very real to you."

I look at the pages that follow. There aren't very many yet, even though I worked all night. I smile at the very first lines of my true story:

George's blue eyes captured her. They were dark as the deep blue sea and Sadie was adrift under a starless night. No going back now.

I love it, cliché and all.

"He is real to me," I say.

"But he's just a story."

I shrug. "'Who's to say that dreams and nightmares aren't as real as the here and now?'"

"Who said that?" she asks. I must have been using my quoting voice.

"John Lennon."

"You know, he also said, 'I get by with a little help from my friends.'"

I roll my eyes.

"What I mean is, it's okay to ask for help too." She glances at the tiny plastic cup on her desk, and my eyes follow hers.

"So we agreed that we'd start with an antidepressant," she begins again. "These pills are not magic, Sadie, and this is a long-term plan. Do you have any more questions about what this medication does?"

I try to remember to be strong. I played through this conversation a lot last night, and I imagined all the things I might say. Imagining something can be a good way to get ready for it.

"If they have to build up in your system and they don't work right away, couldn't you just, like, give me a prescription and then I'd get it filled and all that?" I ask. It turns my stomach to have to do this here and now, like an execution. I can feel the gun to my back. It's like George always says: the most important part of dying is saying goodbye.

"Listen, Sadie. You love a symbol, right? Think of it that way. This symbolizes making a choice. It's a metaphor."

"Except it's also drugs."

"Well, yes," she admits. "Also drugs. You know, you've taken so many big steps here, and I'm so happy that we've managed to start talking about George and your true story. But it's easy to fall back into old habits when you return to your old environment. We'd prefer it if we sent you off on the right foot. Besides, you love a crossroads, don't you? A fork on the highway. 'Two roads diverged in a wood—'"

"And I, I took the road *most* traveled by."

"The traveled path is often the safer one."

I wonder if she's read that poem. It's the road not taken that one regrets.

She's smiling. Does it even matter what the words "really" mean? Or should I just listen to what she's trying to tell me with them? It's hard to interpret a smile. I feel like the Sadie who came into this hospital would have wanted me to say that I feel afraid, but I don't. Her smile doesn't seem sinister. I can't make myself see those things in her anymore.

"What are you thinking?" she asks.

"I don't know," I lie.

"That's not true, but it's okay. I hope you find someone you can trust enough to tell your stories to. I hope you can find someone to take this adventure with."

"I had someone," I say. She shakes her head.

"But that's not real."

"It's real to me." *To George and me,* I think.

"Something can be powerful without being real. You don't think you would be happier living in the real world, instead of in stories and books?"

I shake my head.

"Every story I've ever needed has arrived like . . ." Like what? I think of the Star Palace opening to welcome me. "Like a door at exactly the right time. They became *my* story. It was like reading them made me a different person, like casting a spell over me. And I have no idea why that is . . . some magical combination of time and place, and the characters and the author and the universe . . . and me. What you're making me give up . . ."

"You understand that no one is asking you to give up anything. . . . No one is saying you can never read another book."

"But it won't be the same. It won't be like before."

"You said it yourself. It's a combination of things. You can still read. You can even still imagine things and day-dream. But we want you to be able to live in the real world with everyone out here who cares about you. We want you to walk away from your crash at last."

She hesitates. "But, remember, it's up to you. No one is *making* you do this. Do you want this, or don't you?"

She hands me the cup and sits back in her chair, folding her hands in her lap.

A blue pill rattles around in the bottom of the cup.

"Can I just . . . have a moment?" I ask, holding the cup with both hands.

"Take your time," she says.

I let my eyes wander, and my mind follows. I feel George slip in.

Dr. Roberts won't make me tell her what I see, but I will remember. It will haunt me forever, as it should.

✳

"Cigarette?" George asks.

The palace has succumbed to ruin. Have a hundred years passed in this place, as they would have in Narnia? Is neglect the measure of its years? I imagine him sitting on the edge of our bed, watching the walls crumble around him.

He's packed up his attaché case, which lays open on the floor. It isn't weapons or tools he's packed, but memories: pictures, maps, and treasures. Like he's fleeing.

It makes my heart hurt, seeing what is most precious to him.

"I can't play these games now, George," I say, my throat tight. He shrugs and smiles, his crumpled suit aging rapidly before my eyes. He takes two cigarettes from an ivory box on our nightstand and holds both in his mouth to light them. He gives me one, but I don't raise it to my lips the way I should. I let it sit between my fingers and burn.

George strides over to the balcony in a cloud of sweet-smelling smoke, and when he turns back to me, his smile is as addictive as it was the first instant we met.

"I know you have to leave me now. But this doesn't have to be The End," he says. "We just have to get out of here. Stick to the plan, my spy, my witch, my darling."

I make myself say the words.

"This *is* the end, George. This is it. We can't do this anymore. You are not real, and I am."

He turns away, and though he is perfectly still, I know him too well not to realize that he is crying.

I stand and go to him, but I don't dare touch him; I can't bear it.

"May I visit you?" he asks. "Only sometimes. It won't be often."

"You know you can't. George . . ."

"Please. I'm scared. I'm really scared."

We stand side by side like that for a long time, gazing back into our ruined fortress. For once, real courage is demanded of both of us.

I will give him up, and all the moments we have wasted together will be nothing, because they will be gone. Even the memory will be hidden away: a symptom. The story of us will die as I force myself not to think of him. And I will be half a person. And George will be gone.

That thought echoes in my head. *George will be gone.*

My eyes rest on his attaché case. All the pictures of all our adventures are scattered inside. I long for those moments.

I reach for them, just to touch them one last time. But I stop as something gold on the floor catches my eye. A lovely unbroken gilt frame is peeking out, shoved under the bed. I pick it up. It's a picture that doesn't belong here in the Star Palace. My favorite from Mrs. Vaughn's wall of heroes: Henry, Lucie, and me watching a movie, lit up like ghosts by the glow of the television. It makes me smile. It fills me with warmth when I touch it. I set it on the nightstand. I close George's case, shutting temptation out of sight.

He is shaking. He knows this is the end, because I know. We are standing against the wall, staring into the firing squad, final cigarettes hanging from our lips.

"And will you be happy, Sadie?" His hand can barely hold the cigarette: a firefly of ash flickers and dies. I follow his gaze into the worlds we have built and the infinity of those we will never get to build: all of the worlds I will lose. Their evening lights dance all the way to the horizon, out beyond the seas.

"Oh, George, don't let's ask for the moon," I manage to whisper. "We've had the stars."

He is so still, but smoke escapes his lips, like a dream he's been holding in. I ease myself back into my wheelchair, and the dream dissolves around me, reality closing in. Finally it is just George, and me, and our little pocket out of time. When he turns back to me, he is smiling.

"Goodbye," I say. We keep our eyes fixed on each other. Those eyes like mine: two infinite oceans of possibility.

I close my eyes and force myself to see only the blackness behind my eyelids, nothing more.

I put the plastic cup to my lips.

I make my choice.

And then he is gone.

ACKNOWLEDGMENTS

This book would not have been possible without many incredible people. I would like to thank:

My superlative agent, Lucy Carson; the wonderful Alix Kaye; and friends at the Friedrich Agency.

Wendy Lamb, the best editor I could have dreamed up; my amazing assistant editor, Dana Carey; and friends at Wendy Lamb Books, including designer Angela Carlino, interior designer Jaclyn Whalen, copy editor Colleen Fellingham, managing editor Tamar Schwartz, publicist Kathy Dunn, and the rest of the team at RHCB.

My family, for supporting me.

My friends at American University Library, for their indulgence.

Lindsey and Megan, who read drafts and shared thoughts. Dewey for the wake-up calls. Alex for listening.

Ruth for reading the worst version of this book and burying my frustration in Netrunner.

Finally, my number one reader, Ethan: Your refusal to entertain my endless neuroses made this book possible. Thank you for putting up with all the skulls. Emoji heart.

AUTHOR'S NOTE

The spark for Sadie's story came on a long snowy walk when I was completely lost in thought. I was so deep inside my own head that I didn't even perceive the world around me, and all of a sudden Sadie and George were there. I didn't notice until I got home that my feet had begun to bleed in my boots.

That's not so unusual for writers: I've heard of writers who laugh and cry as they write scenes, who pace relentlessly, who lose hours of time. It's a good thing, usually, to become so absorbed in a story that the real world fades away.

But like anything, it's possible to have too much of a good thing.

Sadie is, in many ways, a writer too. A lot of people who love reading and losing themselves in other worlds will understand exactly what she feels, both good and bad. There's even a growing movement for a name that captures the feeling of becoming too lost in imagination: maladaptive daydreaming.

Daydreams are invisible, and so difficult to explain even to those closest to us, but their seductive draw is universal. I wanted to write a story that takes that need to withdraw into other worlds (and the problems that need can cause) seriously. The allure of the counterfactual tempts everyone, and it's easy to get lost there. If while reading this book you saw yourself in Sadie, I hope you've also come to see: just like Sadie, you are not alone.

ABOUT THE AUTHOR

Tara Wilson Redd, a graduate of Reed College, grew up all over the United States, including in St. Louis, Seattle, and Central Oregon. An impenitent dilettante, she is interested in everything, but especially in language, travel, and animals. When she is home from her adventures, she lives in Washington, DC, where she works in libraries. *The Museum of Us* is her first novel. Visit her online at tarawilsonredd.com.